LEVON'S TIME

Special thanks Jaye Manus and Michael Hutchison
for their always able assistance.

1

Dirya had been walking for years. At least, that was how it felt.

The asphalt under her feet was cold, even with the sun high in the bronze sky. Despite her felt-lined boots, her feet were numb. The boots were tight as well. When they had left Aleppo years before, she was a little girl with a little girl's feet. She was a young woman now, or so her mother would tell her. Her feet had grown as she grew older, and were swollen from the many kilometers she had walked.

Ahead of her and behind stretched a miles-long column of people walking north along the Gaziantep Highway toward the refugee camp at Islahiye. Men and women wore layers against the cold, and were pulling or pushing carts loaded with goods. Walking singly and in bunches, they strung out to the horizon. The smallest children were carried or rode the carts. The older ones walked as Dirya did, not with the springy step of the young, but with the steady trudge of the aged.

The progression passed EkoPet and TurkOil petrol

stations every ten kilometers or so. These were guarded by sullen men standing under hand-painted banners that read TURKS ONLY in Turkish and Arabic. Dirya looked with longing at the coolers of juice and soda visible through the windows of the stations.

Also spaced along the road were army trucks with Turkish soldiers watching the endless parade. Sometimes they waved the walkers along with harsh words and insults. For the most part, they simply glared at the Kurds, Circassians, Yazidis, and Arabs heading to the north along the right lanes of the highway. The soldiers were there to keep them to the path. Anyone who attempted to leave the road, to rest in the shade of trees to the east or west, could expect to be beaten, or worse.

One man stopped to relieve himself in a ditch out of sight of the others. The soldiers hauled him back up onto the asphalt, clubbed him with rifles, and scattered the goods that spilled from the pack on his back. The man rejoined the caravan, whimpering and moaning. No one looked at him or offered to help. Dirya and her mother picked up their pace to leave him behind, both pushing their cart loaded with colorful Carrefour bags to join the next group walking ahead.

The cart they pushed contained all they owned in the world, a collection of clothing and kitchenware and a few packets of family photographs. Buried deep in a bag at the bottom of the heap was a sack of jewelry. It was all that remained of the rings, bracelets, tiaras, and earrings they'd taken from her father's jewelry store at the Shahba Mall in Aleppo. The sack had been heavier when they left. Her mother had had to pay out many of the pieces to get them this far, some of it even to her father's brother in A'zaz, who owned an olive farm and had agreed to keep them until the civil war was over.

But the war had not ended. After two years, her uncle wanted payment in exchange for their board. In addition to the payments, Dirya and her three brothers had to work in the groves. She never wanted to see another olive again. The smell of them turned her stomach.

Armed men from Rojava, a militia opposed to President Assad, came to the farm and drafted all the men, including Dirya's father and brothers. The youngest, Tofan, only eleven, was loaded, shrieking for his mother, into the back of a truck. When the militia had left, her uncle said that she and her mother could no longer stay with him. They began the long hike to the Turkish border and the refugee camp beyond. They could do nothing but survive and pray for the war to end. And wait to be reunited with the men of the family.

The caravan reached a crossroads at a town called Altınüzüm, where there was a collection of trucks and canopies set up by aid organizations. Men and women handed out bottled water and sealed cardboard boxes to a crowd eager to have them. A blonde woman in a red parka gave Dirya and her mother a bag of bread and a small cloth sack of rice, along with a gallon jug of clean water. The woman spoke Arabic with more confidence than skill. Dirya understood little of what she said, but nodded and returned the woman's smile.

Soldiers stood at the blockades guarding the roads that led into the town and smiled as well. They were fixed smiles, empty of good will or humor, but pasted on their faces for the cameras of the media people gathered at the aid stop. There was a dusty van with a satellite dish atop a tower on the roof. Western men and women with serious faces snapped pictures and asked questions through translators. The refugees flocking around the tables of goods being distributed either nodded mutely at the questions or ignored the reporters entirely. These foreigners with their cameras and their questions would be safe in their homes in Belgium or Sweden this time next week. The refugees had to remain, and to speak to outsiders meant drawing attention to themselves—the attention of the watching soldiers.

Dirya and her mother pushed their cart into the shade of some cypress trees to open the boxes given to them by the aid workers. There were sewing kits, washcloths, toilet paper, combs, pens, and small pads of paper, as well as packaged cookies, crackers, and dried fruit. Each of the two boxes also had hand-written notes in western languages. One featured a child's crayon drawing of a dog and a house under a yellow sun. The girl had yellow hair. Her dog was pink. Dirya found it funny that there was also toothpaste and toothbrushes, in addition to the boiled sweets. She said so to her mother as they leaned against their cart, enjoying this brief respite from their march.

As they munched cookies and shared a bottle of water, Dirya watched the news people walking along the line of waiting refugees, poking cameras and microphones at them. Cameramen trotted along the column, recording the suffering for the entertainment of an audience thousands of miles away. Each cameraman had someone moving with them, holding a padded microphone on a pole suspended overhead.

The men and women wore the costume of journalists the world over: vests crammed with gear, sunglasses, ball caps with their channel's logo on them, stylish hiking boots or sneakers, and pleated khakis from the best suppliers. All moved with an urgency that belied the fact that this had been years and years in duration: a slow-motion human catastrophe being hyped for a two-minute segment on the evening news, if it didn't get bumped for a celebrity divorce or a political controversy.

One man was apart from the frantic activity of the others. Dirya noticed him standing in the shade of a canopy slung off one of the aid trucks. He held a steaming mug to warm his hands. He wore a lined fatigue jacket over a faded work shirt, and battered boots with worn soles were visible under the hems of his ACU trousers. A frayed backpack with a Canadian flag stitched on it rested at his feet.

He was a big man with broad shoulders. The canopy's shadow hid his face, but it was clear from his posture that he was watching the column before him, his head turning to regard the trotting cameramen and hectoring reporters. He was a Westerner, but not a reporter or an aid worker. Dirya did not know how she knew this. She was certain this man was here in this place for reasons all his own.

Her attention was drawn away by the arrival of a black SUV that pulled to a stop on the opposite side of the highway. Men in black suits over starched white shirts exited from all four doors. Their jackets were open, revealing holstered weapons on their belts. One of them carried a camera in his hands. This frightened Dirya more than the guns. She'd seen so many men with guns. The black suits walked quickly to the reporters and camera crews working the line. The soldiers by the blockades either looked through them or turned away.

The leader of the new arrivals was a big man with a shaved head. He spoke to one of the journalists, who began to argue with him. It was too far away for Dirya to hear the words, but she could see the younger man's face turning red. The bald man took his hand as if in a friendly grip. The younger man paled, his lips tight, as the bald man leaned closer to speak into his ear. The rest of the men from the SUV stood in a tight row to block the others from recording the scene or hearing what was said.

Dirya turned to where the tall man had been standing in the shade of the canopy. He was gone.

2

"Your closet makes me sad," Sandy Hamer said.

"You only say that 'cause my clothes are too small for you to borrow," Merry Cade said. Sandy was a couple of years older than Merry. The divide felt like an eon at times like this.

They were up in Merry's room on the second floor of Uncle Fern's house. Sandy was bored enough to do an inventory of Merry's wardrobe. She plucked a pair of denim overalls from the closet and dangled them in front of Merry, who was lying on the bed with a paperback.

"Please tell me these are for Halloween." Sandy sighed.

"What am I supposed to wear to clean out stalls? You don't exactly look like the cover of *Elle* when you're shoveling shit for your mom." Merry's gaze returned to the pages of her paperback. Mike Hammer was recovering from a blow to the skull. That was when he did his best detective work, woozy from a concussion.

"Well, I don't dress like a farmer!" With grunts

of disgust, Sandy rifled through more hangers. She plucked out clothes to waggle in the air before putting them back. "Ugh. Ick. Loser. Tomboy."

"I know I need new clothes. My daddy can take me shopping when he comes back." Merry turned a page.

"When's that?" Sandy dropped beside her on the bed.

"Soon. I don't know. He'll be here before Christmas."

"And what? Take you to Walmart? Buy you some more stuff in the boy's department?"

"I pick out my own clothes."

Sandy huffed out her deepest sigh.

"You can't wait that long. Not only is your crap lame, but you're outgrowing it." Sandy plucked at the cuff of one of Merry's jeans legs.

"Not that it matters. Who'll ever see me?"

"And that's another problem. You're either here, or hanging with my mom. No one *ever* sees you. Are you *ever* going to school?"

"I'm homeschooled," Merry said.

"By who? Your uncle? What's he teaching you? How to be a hillbilly?"

Merry sat up with a mock-angry face and delivered a playful punch to Sandy's arm. Sandy stuck out her lip in an exaggerated pout, then leapt from the bed. She skipped back to Merry and yanked the paperback from her hand.

"Come on! Let's go shopping! You and me!" Sandy pulled car keys from her purse, which was hanging on Merry's bedpost. She dangled them before Merry's face.

"In Haley?"

"Sure, in Haley. You have any money?"

"My daddy left me some," Merry said. She thought

of the shoebox on the shelf in the closet and the two coffee cans buried behind Uncle Fern's truck farm, and the one up in the eaves of a stall out in the barn.

"Let's go!"

"Now?"

"*Right* now! Right this damned minute!"

"It's okay with your mom?"

"Sure. She's at the Clarkes' farm. They have two mares ready to foal." Sandy's mother was Jessie Hamer, a long-time friend of Merry's father and the one-woman proprietor of Riverstone Veterinary.

"Well, okay. Go down and tell my Uncle Fern what we're doing, and I'll be right down."

With a yip, Sandy tore from the room and down the steps. Left alone, Merry stood on tiptoes to slide the shoebox from its place above her clothes rack. She set it on the bed and removed the lid. Inside were thick rolls of bills, five in all, bound with rubber bands. She was slipping the bands from one of them when she heard Sandy's booted feet on the stairs.

Merry shoved the shoebox under her pillow. She turned back to the closet to jam a whole roll into the pocket of the parka hanging on a hook on the back of the door.

"First thing we do is replace this ratty old thing," Sandy said, fingering the faux fur lining the parka hood as Merry slid her arms into it.

"Wendy's is on me, okay?" Merry said.

"Sounds like a plan. This will be fun!" Sandy beamed at her.

3

Gunny Leffertz said:
"Sometimes ·oing the right thing is the wrong thing."

Her mother complained of stomach cramps. Dirya suspected the raisin cookies from the aid package. They hadn't eaten anything richer than rice and dried peas for almost a week. Her mother leaned on the cart, face pinched in pain.

"There are toilets," Dirya said.

There were three porta-potties set up behind one of the aid trucks.

"There is a line," her mother protested.

"You must go."

"I cannot leave you alone."

"And I cannot leave the cart."

Her mother suggested going into the copse of cypress that stood beyond the road, but Dirya dissuaded her. The soldiers were watching.

"I will be fine here. There are people everywhere," Dirya said. She gestured at the cameras and reporters.

Her mother nodded once, took the packet of toilet paper from the aid package, and joined the line of two dozen people waiting for the toilets.

Dirya sipped cold tea and watched the parade of refugees file past her toward the impromptu aid station at the crossroads. Her gaze avoided the man in the black suit snapping pictures of new arrivals. He paid particular interest to men of military age, making some of them stop their progress to allow him to get a better shot of their faces. The soldiers stepped closer to give his orders weight.

The journalists were finally satisfied with the footage they got and packed themselves and their equipment into their van and drove off. Dirya looked at the line in front of the toilets but could no longer see her mother there. The column of approaching refugees was thinning now. The day was coming to an end, the shadows getting longer. In this flat, featureless country, sundown was a sudden event. The winter moon was already visible on the horizon. Many had stopped to make camp on the road verge.

She started as she saw the shadow of someone approaching her—the man with the camera. He was smiling, the camera held up and clicking. He was clean-shaven and younger than the other men who had climbed out of the SUV. He might have been handsome but for a mouthful of crooked teeth exposed by his grin.

"You are a Kurd," he said.

Dirya understood enough Turkish to understand him but feigned ignorance.

"You are a guest in my country, see?"

She turned away.

The Turk grabbed her arm, his smile gone.

"And how will you repay that generosity?" His grip tightened.

Dirya looked at the toilets to find her mother. She looked at the aid workers, who were all occupied greeting newcomers. The thinning column of arrivals did not pay her any attention.

"Do not talk. Do not cry out. I saw you with your mother. Filthy Kurd whore, and her filthy Kurd whore daughter. Where are your men?"

She turned to answer but swallowed the words. The grip on her arm tightened and the Turk pulled her toward the trees, the shadows darker there. She saw the bald man and the others smoking, standing by the SUV. One of them called out to the Turk who was dragging her by the arm. A harsh bark from the bald man silenced the speaker.

Dirya stumbled over a tree root, and the Turk hauled her upright with a curse. They were soon out of sight of the road. He pushed her against the bole of a tree, his heavier body against hers, trapping her. His hand went to the hem of her skirts and jerked them up to allow his hand to touch her leg. His other hand opened her coat, tearing away a button in his haste. She turned her head from him, eyes closed, lips pressed tight.

"Do not worry, little one. I do not wish to kiss you." He gave a dry chuckle in his throat as his hand climbed the inside of her thigh, fingers cold against her flesh. His voice was husky with excitement, face greasy with sweat despite the cold. Her nose filled with the rancid smell of his breath: cigarettes and garlic. His hand pressed her thigh, opening her legs wider.

And suddenly he was gone. Dirya sagged to the ground, his weight lifted from her. She opened her eyes to see the Turk on the ground. The tall man she'd seen before bent over him. The tall man had the Turk's shirt front balled in his fist and was repeatedly slamming the heel of his hand into the other man's face. The Turk's face was a mask of blood now. A few of his teeth glistened wetly on the cypress needles that blanketed the ground.

The tall man crouched by the now-still Turk. He wiped bloody hands on the tail of the Turk's shirt before opening the camera and removing the SD card, which he broke between his fingers.

"Go to your mother," the tall man said in perfectly accented Kurdish. He had the face of a warrior, with a light-colored beard and long-healed scars along his brow ridges. But the eyes beneath the brows were kind.

Dirya started to say something, to give words of thanks.

"Go," he said. A command now.

She ran, throat tight and eyes beginning to sting with tears.

4

"This isn't the way to Walmart," Merry said.

"We're not going to Walmart," Sandy replied.

The minivan turned onto the south ramp for the Huntsville Highway.

"Where are we going, then?"

"The outlet mall. Get you some decent clothes."

"How far is it?" Merry gripped the handle on the door as they came down off the ramp, but Sandy was a better driver than a rider. There was snowmelt on the road surface. The Kia slid in behind a semi, then slipstreamed to the middle lane and around a long truck. Sandy was talking the whole time.

"...and a winter coat that doesn't look like you found it behind a dumpster. You remembered to bring some money, right?"

"Uh-huh." Merry's fingers squeezed the fat wad of bills in her pocket.

"How much?"

"Enough, I think. We'll be back for dinner, right?" Sandy laughed.

An hour later, they pulled into the mall lot under

a gray winter sky that promised snow. Merry could taste it, the sharp tang of the dry air. They drove through the lot, passing brightly lit stores with their brand logos until Sandy found a parking spot less than a dozen slots from the main entrance.

Inside the mall, Merry trotted behind Sandy, the older girl's bootheels clicking on the tiles with each long-legged stride. Merry paused to look at the mall directory, a sprawling map that looked like a salamander redrawn as a geometric design with side corridors leading to endcap stores off the broad main building. Sandy called for her to catch up. They started at one end and worked their way through one clothing store after another. Sandy talked Merry into trying on some clothes she'd never consider wearing in public. They argued back and forth, with Sandy pushing for the wild and impractical and slutty. Merry was staying with more sensible outfits.

"You're like an old lady!" Sandy complained.

"My daddy says I was born old."

It was like dress-up until Sandy told Merry to get serious. The store staff was eyeing the giggling pair at each stop. A clerk at a shoe store was losing patience with them until she caught a glimpse of Merry's pimp roll. Sandy's eyes went wide too, her mouth dropping open in wonder.

Outside, back in the mall proper, Sandy could no longer contain herself.

"Did your dad win the lottery?" she squealed in a stage whisper.

"He didn't know how long he'd be gone," Merry said. She thought back to the remaining four rolls in the shoebox in her room.

"Are they *all* twenties?"

"I don't know. I didn't look at all of them." Merry removed the roll from her coat pocket, only to have Sandy clamp her hands around it to hide it.

"Let's keep that out of sight, okay?"

Merry nodded and returned the cash to her pocket.

They had two large bags of tops, skirts, a sweater, jeans, belts, and a pair of alligator cowboy boots that Sandy said made Merry look like Taylor Swift. Merry wanted to get something to eat, but Sandy insisted on one more store. Just one.

In a large outlet box store, they squeezed through aisles of coats carrying the bulging bags.

"We're going to find something right for you and *burn* this thing," Sandy said, giving the sleeve of Merry's parka a tug.

"I like this," Merry said. She pulled a dark-maroon wool coat from the rack and held it against her.

"Nice, if you're buying it for Grandma," Sandy remarked.

Merry turned to a mirror, holding the coat in front of her. Sandy flushed and held a hand to her chin.

"I'm so sorry, Merry."

"It's okay. You were just making a joke. You really think this looks too old for me?"

Merry had shared part of her life with Sandy, but not all of it. Like her father's connection to the death of her maternal grandmother, and the disappearance of her grandfather. Grandmother Roth had been killed by men looking for her father. A lot of those men were dead now, along with a bunch of other men over the past few years, as Levon Cade and his daughter went on the run to escape the consequences of the trouble her father had gotten into. She'd never know all of it, and what she knew would be a secret she would keep to the grave. But she needed to share some of it, even obliquely, with someone else. In late-night gab sessions, Merry had let Sandy into her life. In person. Never on the phone. Never in texts or emails. She was her father's little girl and knew firsthand the dangers loose talk could call down on them. She'd only recently escaped the "care" of the government.

Sandy brightened. "What about something in leather?" She took Merry by the wrist and led her to racks of leather coats in all kinds of shades with fur collars and paisley quilt or cushy lamb linings. These were high-ticket items secured to the racks by slim steel chains run through the right sleeve of each garment.

"Did you see these price tags?" Merry asked.

"You can afford it, girl. Y'all are rich," Sandy said.

Could she? Was she? This money, and the rest hidden around her uncle's farm, had been left for her to use in her father's absence. To help Fern and take care of her needs. Neither of them knew how long that would be, or if her father would ever return from Iraq. She tried not to think about that. She had spent many days and nights trying not to think about it. She'd grown up with that fear, and couldn't remember a time when she didn't have it somewhere in the back of her mind. It was exhausting. Wearing.

A metallic snapping sound took her from these thoughts. Sandy was at the next rack gushing over a shorty jacket trimmed in rabbit fur. The snap and click again. It was coming from the other side of the rack she was standing near.

Merry slipped around the corner of the rack to peek at the gap between the coats and the wall of the dressing rooms. A dark-haired girl in a flowered dress crouched there, cutting the security chains with a pair of tin snips. She was smaller than Merry, with hollow cheeks and a pronounced chin. Merry couldn't see the girl's eyes, but her skin was brown like milky tea. Her arms were skinny, and she was having trouble working the snips through the fine chain links. She freed a pair of coats from their hangers, folded them, and stuffed them into a large Tommy Hilfiger bag.

Retreating as quietly as she could, Merry waited until the girl had slipped from the hiding place and moved across the store. She caught a glimpse of the girl's face in a mirror as she passed it on the way to the main corridor. Large dark eyes staring unblinkingly ahead. She was a pretty girl, but her looks were marred by tightly-pressed lips; her face showed strain.

"Let's go," Merry said. She yanked Sandy by the arm.

"Hold on! Hold on!" Sandy gathered up the bags to follow her friend through the store.

Merry kept the girl in sight, staying behind her in the crowd of shoppers as the girl exited the store into the main mall. Merry crossed the broad corridor to follow at an angle. Sandy, breathing hard, caught up with her.

"What the hell, Merry?" She tried to hand off one of the bulky bags to Merry, who ignored her, eyes fixed ahead.

"That girl stole some coats."

"What girl?"

"Flowered dress. Tommy Hilfiger bag. Two o'clock."

Sandy was confused, so Merry had to point. The girl was moving swiftly, dodging around shoppers walking with snacks or bags.

"She's a shoplifter?" Sandy asked.

"She's got about four thousand dollars' worth of merchandise in that bag."

"So tell Security. Or ignore it."

"I want to follow her."

"Say what, now?" Sandy broke into a trot to keep up. Merry re-crossed the corridor as the girl with the Hilfiger bag turned into the food court.

5

Gunny Leffertz said:
"Sometimes it's how har♦ you can get hit."

Levon was helping the bleeding man to his feet when Baldy and the others came trotting through the trees. They had drawn their pistols and trained them on Levon.

They barked orders at him. He shrugged, palms up in the universal gesture of not understanding the language. Baldy stepped forward to take the bleeding man's arm and pull him clear of Levon. After a swift kick from another guy to the back of Levon's knee, he dropped to the ground on all fours.

Baldy growled questions at his dazed comrade. The guy was struggling to maintain consciousness, his slurred speech coming through torn lips. Blood-flecked spittle sprayed from a fresh gap between his front teeth. The guy's eyes rolled up white, and he slumped to a heap at Baldy's feet.

"Look, it was a misunderstanding, okay?" Levon said. A kick took him in the side. He rolled away from it, and another foot came down to stomp on his knee. He made an attempt to rise, holding a hand out to ask them to let him up. A foot on his shoulder tumbled him over. He moved his head in time to take only a glancing blow from a heel across his face.

He'd let them work him over for a while; anything to delay the story of the girl being told. Let them think it was just between him and the snaggle-toothed guy. Allow the girl and her mother to get away down the road. One of them took him by the hair, spit in his face, and called Levon some bad names he recognized, followed by what were probably dire promises of future punishment. The others were engaged in a heated discussion over the still form of their pal, probably talking about whether to get him medical care or keep working the *yabanci* over.

They compromised, forming a circle to kick Levon's back, sides, shoulders, and ass. He stayed balled up with his legs pressed tightly together and head bent forward into the crook of his arms, fingers splayed across the back of his neck. They did this until they were all winded. One of them bent over with a wracking smoker's cough.

A knee landed on his back, then his wrists were pulled behind him, and cuffs snapped in place. Rough hands lifted him from the dust to walk-march him back toward the road. Two others had their pal by the elbows and mostly carried him back to their SUV. They bundled Levon into the back seat, banging his head on the doorjamb on the way in. Snickers all around.

One of the human rights workers fast-walked toward them, holding up a smartphone. Baldy met him halfway, shoving him before yanking the phone from his hand. The phone was dashed to the roadway and crushed under Baldy's heel. A stream of curses and a second shove sent the Samaritan retreating back to his truck.

In the back, a man was seated either side of him, both smaller than Levon and suddenly conscious of it. There was no room in the front seat for Baldy, so he stood on the running board in the open passenger-side door and banged the roof to signal the driver to take off. He clung there, Mussolini-style, as the SUV spun around and headed toward the town spread out above the highway.

Levon lifted his head enough to look past one of the thugs. Beyond the trucks at the intersection, the highway was empty of foot traffic. The girl and her mama were over the horizon.

6

"I thought you were hungry?" Sandy asked. She'd returned to their table with slices of pizza and Cokes that Merry didn't even touch.

"That girl is with some older men,' Merry said. Their table provided a vantage point from which Merry could see across the open food court to where the dark-eyed girl sat in a booth with a pair of men. One was a heavy-set guy in a tight-fitting red jacket with the Dos Equis logo in a stripe down the sleeves. The second was a younger guy in a black t-shirt meant to show off prison muscles covered in a dense tapestry of tattoos. Both men sported short-back-and-sides haircuts that left a bushy strip of jet-black hair atop their heads. They were as dark as the girl.

"Probably relatives. Maybe her dad." Sandy jabbed a long straw into the ice of her drink and squinted at the booth, which was visible over the fronds of plastic plants under a faux atrium roof.

"No. The body language is all wrong."

"What does that even mean?"

"Eat your pizza and let me watch."

"I'm eating your pizza, too."

"Help yourself. Don't care." Merry watched the drama playing out. She was right that the girl was scared, and not of getting caught stealing. She was afraid of these two. The older man stabbed a finger at her, his mouth twisting as he spoke. The younger man tilted his head to poke around the Hilfiger bag, which was now under the table. He looked at the tags with an appraising eye. The two men had the remnants of a meal before them, paper plates, crushed napkins, and drink cups. The girl's eyes moved from the older man's face to the remaining fries lying atop an open sandwich wrapper. The men offered her nothing.

"Mmmm, pepperoni," Sandy said. Merry cut her a look and went back to surveillance.

The girl slid from the booth to stand, her back to Merry. The older man scowled up at her and handed her a folded shopping bag. She took it in her arms, nodding to the man. He waggled his fingers at her, shooing her away. The girl turned to go, unfolding the bag, this one from The Gap, as she returned to the mall. She looked around as she moved between the tables to exit the food court. Her eyes met Merry's for a split second. Merry had never seen eyes so sad and bereft of hope. The girl moved as a ghost might among the living, part of the world but invisible, intangible.

"Go to the car, and I'll call you," Merry said, standing up from the table.

"What what what?" Sandy asked around a mouthful of crust and cheese.

"Take the bags. Go to the car. Wait for me to call you." Merry turned to run after the girl, who was now joining the flow of foot traffic heading for the west end of the mall.

The girl kept walking, the empty Gap bag dangling free in one hand. Her face was raised to read the colorful logos above each storefront. She paused by a kiosk selling fresh-baked pretzels. Merry feigned interest in the selection of sunglasses at another kiosk, keeping an eye on the girl in a mirror. The girl was on the move again, and Merry followed until she turned to enter an American Eagle store.

Sliding between the racks of flannels and khakis, Merry stopped beside a rack of lumberjack shirts to watch the girl moving between tables stacked with folded jeans. She was studying the labels, looking for whatever the fat man in the jacket had told her to find.

"Can ah help you?"

Merry turned to a rangy girl with blue hair, a nametag that said her name was Cyrise pinned to a t-shirt that announced she was SUPER GAY. The salesgirl was only a few years older than Merry, but her attitude suggested that she was drunk on the limited authority granted her by American Eagle. She made it clear that she did not approve of unattended kids wandering around her shop.

"I'm looking for something," Merry said. She turned her eyes from the sad-eyed girl, who was now rooting through the high stacks of jeans.

The salesgirl snorted. "That's specific."

"These shirts are nice." Merry fingered one of the flannels.

"Those are men's shirts."

"I didn't think that mattered. You know?" Merry gestured at the salesgirl's shirtfront.

Cyrise's lip curled.

"You know, like *your* shirt," Merry continued.

The salesgirl looked down at her own shirt. Merry

glanced past her to see the little shoplifter lowering a short stack of jeans into her Gap bag. The salesgirl sighed and tilted her head with an eye roll.

"They make us wear this. It's part of a promotion to show the store's support of the Pride community."

"Uh-huh."

"I'm not gay, but it'd be okay if I was, right?"

"Uh-huh. That's great. Thank you." Merry walked away, leaving the salesgirl staring behind her.

The sad-eyed girl was out of American Eagle now and into the main corridor again. She turned right rather than left. Her path led away from the food court toward a destination in the west end of the mall. There were more items on her shoplifting list.

The phone in Merry's jeans pocket buzzed and shuddered. She pulled it out and opened it. It was the last flip-phone in the civilized world, according to Sandy.

"Are you in the parking lot?" Merry said, talking as she walked.

"I'm in the car. What the hell?" Sandy's voice rose an octave as she spoke.

"Head for the entrance between Johnny Rockets and Reebok."

"Where is that?"

"Just drive around till you see it and park at the curb."

"How do *you* know where it is? You've never been here before."

"I looked at the directory."

"Yeah, for like a second."

"Just do it, Sandy."

"Okay, Nancy Drew. Oh—"

Merry snapped the phone closed and replaced it in

her pocket. The girl was fifty feet ahead of her, standing at the opening to a Calvin Klein store. Merry picked up the pace and caught up with her as she stepped toward the security detectors. For the first time, Merry wondered how the girl was getting past the panels that broke each store entrance into chutes. Each store had them, yet the girl sailed through without setting them off.

The girl's head snapped around when Merry took her wrist. Her eyes went saucer-wide. The muscles held in Merry's grip tightened.

"*¿Quieres venir conmigo?*" Merry asked.

The girl's eyes looked past Merry. A pair of security guards, a man and a woman, stood speaking before a coffee kiosk. They wore white uniform shirts with the gaudy mall logo on the shoulders. Belts sagged under the weight of radio equipment, mace canisters, and stun guns.

"*No los mires. Quieres ·ejar aqui. ¿Quieres venir conmigo?*" Merry said, strengthening her grip on the girl's wrist.

The girl looked at her, then back down the mall corridor, eyes searching the approaching shoppers.

When the girl's gaze returned to her, Merry said, "*Esos hombres no te encontrarán si nos vamos ahora.*"

The girl was panting now, her throat quivering rapidly. Her pupils were practically twirling in her head as she weighed the unexpected range of options suddenly presented to her.

"Come on," Merry said. She yanked the girl's wrist, and together they moved at a fast walk toward the next bisecting corridor and the northwest exit.

7

"What is your name?"

"William Brett Hogue," Levon lied.

"That is what it says on your passport."

"Because that's my name," Levon said.

"You are Canadian?"

"Yes. Moosejaw, Saskatchewan," Levon lied again.

"Mooze-chaw?"

"Yes."

The bald man had removed his black jacket. He wiped sweat from his scalp with a hand towel offered him by a subordinate, then leaned on the table and fixed Levon with his gaze. Levon sat opposite with his wrists cuffed behind him, the chain threaded through the bars of a steel chair.

The room was a windowless cell in the basement of the Altınüzüm police station. They'd stripped him down to his boxers. His clothing and the contents of his rucksack were spread out on a second table. His back and ribs were covered with red bruises, which were turning blue. They'd tuned him up more on the ride here, an expert but perfunctory job. They'd made certain not to strike his face, but for that one sidelong kick. It didn't hurt when he breathed, so he knew his ribs were intact. There'd be blood when he pissed; he was sure of that.

"You are spy. You work for the opposition," Baldy said. He meant anyone who didn't agree with Erdo an, the current president.

"I work with Care-Euro," Levon lied. It was a humanitarian organization based in Brussels.

"That is what your papers say, but they have never heard of you, William Hogue."

It was Baldy's turn to lie. Levon was sure that Care-Euro didn't have a comprehensive list of all its volunteers. And they'd never share it with the Turkish secret police, even if they did. He was certain that was who was dealing with. The *Millî* İstihbarat *Teşkilâtı.* The signature black suits gave them away. The real success of a secret police that wants to oppress a population is to make them not a secret at all. These guys operated in plain sight to make arrests and hold suspects indefinitely as authorized by the National Assembly in Ankara. And, since Erdoğan had the assembly in a stranglehold, they were the president's bully boys at home and abroad.

"Maybe my paperwork is still moving through channels," Levon said.

"You think because you are a foreigner, a Westerner, it gives you special privileges. You can assault a policeman with immunity?" He probably meant impunity. His English was excellent otherwise, spoken with a distinct Harrow accent.

"He was raping a little girl."

"He was interrogating a suspect!" Baldy slammed the table with the flat of his hand. The resulting boom made his subordinate leap in response.

"I'd like to speak to someone at the Canadian consulate," Levon said.

"You will speak to no one until you tell me the truth, William Hogue. Until you admit to me that you are not Canadian. You are not a volunteer. You are not William Hogue. Until then, you are a spy working against the legitimate government of my country and will be held in secret, tried in secret, and imprisoned in secret."

"You're going to be sorry when Ottawa hears about this."

Baldy's face flushed purple.

"Fuck your Ottawa!" He reached across the table, and this time, the flat of his hand struck Levon. Anticipating the blow, Levon ducked his head while turning his face away. The policeman's fingers struck the hardest part of Levon's skull. It stung enough to make Baldy wince.

"I want to speak to my consulate," Levon said.

Baldy made a fist, and the flesh around his lips turned white. He turned and walked from the cell, leaving his subordinate uncertain of what to do. Finally, the man followed his superior from the room, leaving Levon alone in the cell to weigh his meager options.

8

"What are we doing? What are we doing here? What are we *actually* doing?" Sandy was panicking as she piloted the minivan north on Huntsville Highway through beep-and-creep traffic.

In the rear seat, the dark-eyed girl was uttering a stream of rapid-fire prayers or apologies or who knew what. Merry couldn't follow most of it.

"I was right. Those guys aren't related to her," Merry said. She was turned in her seat, watching the girl rock back and forth, tears in her eyes. Her little hands clutched the crumpled Gap bag like a life preserver.

"You got that from what she's saying? I had three years of Spanish, and it sounds like blah blah blah to me!"

"She told me in the parking lot while we were waiting for you."

"How can you understand her?"

"Homeschooling."

"Who taught *you Español*? Uncle Fern?"

Merry shrugged. "Univision. Telemundo. I just learned it."

Traffic was picking up. The wipers slapped back and forth against the salty slush sprayed on the windshield by passing trucks. Sandy took a deep breath, let it out, and forced her hands to relax on the wheel. They hurt from the white-knuckle grip she'd been maintaining since they'd pulled off the outlet lot.

"So, what are we doing with her? You can't just kidnap someone," Sandy said. Her voice had returned to normal, along with her breathing. Her fingers tapped the wheel.

"Those two kidnapped her. Or bought her like a slave. I'm not sure yet." Merry watched the blue road signs for the next exit go by.

"We need to take her to the police," Sandy said.

"We're not doing that. Not until we know more."

"Up to this moment, we haven't done anything wrong."

"She could accuse us of helping her shoplift."

"Well, she's not coming to my house!" Sandy squeaked. She was strangling the steering wheel again.

"Take the next exit, Sandy." Merry pointed at the exit lane to the right.

"So, we're turning her in?"

"No. I'm hungry, and so is she. There's a Wendy's off this exit."

* * *

They couldn't help but stare at the girl as she packed away two doubles with cheese, a cup of chili, all of her fries, and half of Merry's. She was working on her second Frosty.

"When's the last time she ate?" Sandy asked.

"Look at her. She hasn't had regular meals in a long while," Merry said. She pushed her fry carton closer to the girl, who nodded her thanks.

"Or she's sick."

"No one who's sick eats like that, Sandy. Those two men have been treating her like a stepchild."

"All right. But what are we gonna do? I mean, with *her*?" Sandy nodded toward the girl.

"Drop her off with me. I'll tell Uncle Fern something."

"That she followed you home? She's not a puppy."

"I'll tell him the truth, then."

"And he'll be okay with that? Having an illegal for a sleepover? Breaking the law?"

"Breaking the law's nothing new for the Cades," Merry replied.

The straw in the Frosty croaked and squeaked as the girl went for the dregs. Merry touched her hand gently. The girl looked up; she had a ketchup mustache smeared on her upper lip. Merry handed her a napkin and mimed wiping her mouth. The girl's face darkened. She took the napkin and cleaned her mouth and chin.

"*Mas?* Um, *mas* Frosty?" Merry said.

"*No mas. Muchas gracias.*" A smile quivered at the corner of her mouth.

"I hate to say this, but she smells, too," Sandy said, nose wrinkled.

"God knows how she's been living. That dress isn't helping." The print dress was stained dark under the armpits and at the neck.

"Plus, it's out of season, and two sizes too big," Sandy said, with ever the eye for fashion.

"She's only a size smaller than me. Go out to the car and get her a pair of jeans and that sweater. I'll take her to the ladies' room to wash up."

"If only to make the rest of the ride home bearable,"

Sandy agreed. She slid from the booth and went out to the lot. The girl turned, nervous, not sure why the taller *gringa* was leaving.

"*¿Bano? ¿Lávate? ¿Jabón?*" Merry asked.

The girl blushed again, and she nodded.

Merry cleared the table and threw out their cups and wrappers. The girl followed her to the ladies' room, where Merry showed her to a stall with a toilet and sink. Merry mimed stripping off the dress and washing. She gave the girl her comb.

The girl was in the stall running water when Sandy entered with one of the bags from the outlet. The girls picked out jeans, a belt, and the sweater. Also, a pair of sneakers to replace the sandals the girl wore. They didn't have socks, but the sneakers would do to cover her feet.

"They had her dressed for the beach in December," Sandy said as Merry handed the clothes over the stall door.

"So she couldn't run away. Probably never seen snow and ice in her life," Merry said.

They waited, listening to the water run and the toilet flush. Neither entirely covered the stifled sobs. The girl exited the stall looking like a different person in the colorful print sweater, crisp new denims, and bright white New Balance sneakers. Her face and hands were clean, and her hair was combed back. She had a shy smile on her face, although her eyes were red from crying. She was holding the flowered dress and sandals in her hand.

"Oh, you want to trash those, honey," Sandy said, fingers pinching her nose. Merry gestured to the trash bin under the towel dispenser. The girl stuffed the dress and sandals inside.

They walked out into the chill night air. The girl was startled when Sandy used her remote to unlock the minivan and the lights came on. Sandy, then Merry, laughed before the girl joined in, a hand covering her mouth. Merry slid the bay door of the van open for her.

"*Mi nombre es Merry. Mi amiga es San•y ¿Cómo te llamas?*"

The girl looked from one to the other as Sandy helped her belt herself in.

"Esperanza," she replied.

"Esperanza. That means 'hope,'" Merry said.

"Even I remember *that* much from class," Sandy grumbled. "And we're going to need all we can get."

9

Levon's trial was secret and brief.

He was charged with espionage, terrorism, interfering with an officer of the state, assault, and conspiring to overthrow the legitimate government of Turkey. He had no legal representation and exercised his only recourse, a repeated request to speak to someone at the Canadian consulate.

They'd returned his clothes to him, minus the contents of his pockets. His excellent but fraudulent identification papers were gone, along with his clasp knife, wallet, wristwatch, and cash. They'd also taken his boots and replaced them with a pair of hemp-soled cloth slippers. They allowed him to keep his belt, although they'd slit open the leather to find the gold maple leaf Canadian coins hidden between the layers. These convinced them that he might just be Canadian, as he claimed. An expensive ruse.

His wrists were cuffed to a broad leather belt cinched in place around his waist and secured at the back. Thin steel cables connected the belt to manacles on his ankles through metal rings.

His plea to contact his consulate was translated for the judge, who informed Levon through a translator that he would be allowed to speak to a representative of his government once it was established that he was no longer a threat to the state.

"How do I establish that?" Levon asked.

The translator conferred with the judge and came back with, "When you provide the court with the names of the others in your network of conspirators."

"I wasn't part of a conspiracy. I don't know any names to give you."

Whispered conversation at the bench. A blue-uniformed guard yawned from his seat in a corner of the room. The judge cut him a glare of annoyance.

"That is what a spy, terrorist, and enemy of the state could be expected to say."

"So, it's a Catch Twenty-two."

The translator blinked.

"A paradox. A self-contradictory idea," Levon explained.

The translator nodded once and relayed this to the judge. He came back with, "Until you cooperate, you can expect no further consideration from this court."

"Can I at least ask how long my sentence is to be?"

"That is entirely in your hands."

"And what if I offer no cooperation at all?"

Buzzing at the bench. The judge's frown deepened. He turned his unblinking gaze upon Levon. The translator offered, "Then you will die in Tekirdağ."

The trial was over.

* * *

Three guards came to his cell in the morning. They secured him once again in cuffs, belt, and leg manacles before shoving him onto a raised stool. Two of them watched, hands on truncheons, while the third shaved Levon bald with electric clippers. They left his facial hair. The beard he had grown for protective camouflage remained in place. The scalp job was probably to differentiate him as a prisoner since he still wore the clothes he was arrested in. It wasn't about lice, because they left the beard. Touching a man's beard was serious business in this part of the world.

He was led in a shuffle down steps at the back of the courthouse to a blue bus waiting in an enclosed courtyard. It was cold enough out for him to see his breath, but the inside of the bus was warm. A rich fug of sweat, urine, and tobacco hung in the air from the rows of men seated on wooden benches along either wall.

A pair of guards shoved Levon onto a bench and secured his manacles to ring bolts in the floor. The guards left the prisoners, six in addition to Levon, sitting in the gloom of the windowless bus. There was room for more men, and it looked like they would be waiting until the ride was full.

The other men were dark. Turks or Arabs. The man directly across from Levon stared with one good eye. The other was swollen shut from a very severe and recent beating. The "no faces" rule didn't apply to locals.

"Hamerican?" One-Eye asked.

"Canadian," Levon said. He met the man's gaze.

One-Eye looked perplexed. He elbowed the man next to him. The man shrugged.

"Canadian. Hockey. Tim Horton's."

One-Eye's face twisted in a scowl. He hawked loudly and spit a gobbet of phlegm, which landed between

Levon's feet.

Levon kept eye contact with him while retreating mentally into a fugue state. It was too early to make enemies. Levon gave the man nothing, his gaze steady but neither threatening nor fearful. One-Eye lost interest and turned away to speak to his neighbor. Turkish wasn't a language Levon was fluent in, and One-Eye was a Cypriot with a thick dialect. He could follow it enough to understand that One-Eye thought that the "Hamerican's" chances of being murdered within a week at Tekirdağ were strong. His chance of being raped in the ass was even stronger. This caused snickers from the others.

Levon feigned oblivious disinterest. They were all chained to rings in the floor. No one would be moving on him for the moment. Levon let himself fall deeper into his resting state, simultaneously wakeful but disengaged.

He thought back over the previous week. In theory, crossing into Turkey over the Syrian border had been a sound tactic. He could fit into the flood of refugees as just another foreign humanitarian worker. It had been a better option than slipping over the border from Iraq after leaving Mosul. That part of the plan had worked to perfection. He had melted into the throng with barely a glance from the border guards, who were overwhelmed with processing the mobs of civilians eager to escape the civil war to the south. They were looking for young Arabic and Kurdish men of a certain dangerous age to pull aside. The Arabs because they could be members of Daesh, or ISIS, as the Americans called it. The Kurds because they were Kurds. The white guy with the Canuck flag on his backpack was waved through without a blink.

In hindsight, it had all gone to hell when he saw the girl being taken away to be raped. She reminded him of Merry. He *coul•* have turned away. *Maybe* he could have if he were another kind of man. He was following the snaggle-toothed bastard into the trees before he even knew what he was doing. He knew, before closing with the man, to remove the automatic concealed under his shirt and throw it deep into the woods.

He waited by the man he had dropped until his comrades came to get him and offered no resistance. The rapist was unconscious, and couldn't offer any details. The delay allowed the girl to find her mother and get far away. It had cost him a beating, but that was better than seeing that girl's face for the rest of his life. He didn't need that in his head. He had enough company in there.

A jerk and a tug brought him back to the here and now. The bus was moving. The benches either side had been filled with two dozen new convicts. Sweating men pressed close on either side of him; the benches were at capacity. Two men sat on the floor of the bus, steel cables looped through their wrist chains and locked into ring bolts they shared with seated prisoners.

Some of the new guys were of a different breed than the rest of the passengers. Two wore what looked like expensive Italian-cut suits. These guys were having trouble keeping the fear from their eyes. Another guy was in tan military fatigues. Young guy in his late twenties. Short-cropped hair, and the black mustache that was standard issue in the Turk army. Former military. These were certainly political prisoners. Erdoğan wasn't resting easy in the presidential palace and was locking up anyone not one hundred percent in his corner. That was how Levon had gotten scooped up. This was what justice looked like in a counter-insurgency.

One-Eye made remarks to the two men in suits that caused the other convicts to laugh. One of the men tried to engage One-Eye in a civil conversation that the Cypriot wasn't having any part of. He made further remarks about the two frightened men that caused more laughter. Rather than discourage the hilarity, the guard watching them from a cage behind the driver joined in with his own witticisms. Levon couldn't follow most of it but understood that the harder men were imagining the two suits joining a harem once they got where they were going.

All attention was focused away from him. Levon retreated into himself once again, imagining the rocking of the bus to be the motion of a fishing boat cruising an inlet under a gull-filled sky.

10

It was the best job he'd ever had in his life, and he'd had some shitty jobs.

There weren't a whole lot of cushy gigs for a twenty-nine-year-old with one year of community college. Ed Nunez had flipped burgers and come home smelling of fry grease. His mom made him strip his clothes off in the garage before she'd let him into the house. He did day labor at construction sites and woke up each morning with pain in every joint. When he did restock at the Walmart, then the Target, then the Publix, he realized that dying of boredom was a real possibility.

But working Security at the outlets was a trip, man. The pay was good. The benefits were better. He got to wear a uniform and carry a taser and had a membership at Anytime Fitness paid for by the company. Got to stay fit, right? And staying fit was like a second job with all the free food he got from vendors. He needed four hours a week on the stair-stepper just to burn off all the gratis Cinnabons.

The respect was cool, too. The uniform and the

badge and the taser made people look at him as an adult for the first time in his life. People older than him called him "sir." He could talk to girls he'd never have approached before. The uniform gave him an excuse, opened the world to him in a way that the old Eddie Nunez could never access.

It made him wonder what a *real* cop's life was like. How sweet must that be? He fantasized about maybe stepping up his exercise regime, getting in shape and applying to the sheriff's department. Wear a real uniform. Carry a gun, dude. Drive a police cruiser instead of the piece-of-shit Impreza the mall had him use to patrol the lot.

Not that Ed had any interest in serving the public or the lofty notion of justice. His notion of law and order, right and wrong, was malleable at best. He'd stolen stuff at every job he'd ever worked. Even as a day laborer, he had boosted an air compressor and sold it to his cousin for two bills. He'd never been caught, so he had no record. The mall would never have hired him for this job if he had.

No, for Ed, the authority that the uniform gave him was a gateway to status, however limited, and advantage, like free snack food, and the esteem that gave him the confidence to talk to the fine honeys who worked the store counters and kiosks.

"I'm on break," he told the two guys who slid into the booth opposite him at the food court. The *bonita* at the China Wok had given him an extra-generous helping of kung pao over his rice noodles, and he was anxious to dig in. Walking ten miles a shift worked up an appetite.

But these two guys were serious.

"I want to talk to you," the chubby one said. The

other one, a tatted-up younger dude, just stared. He had a thick accent like Ed's *abuela*. Ed peppered his speech with phrases his grandparents used but was hardly bilingual.

"Yeah?" Ed said, taking up a forkful of spicy noodles.

"E. Nunez," the chubby guy read from plastic name badge on the breast of Ed's uniform blouse. "Ernesto? Enrique?"

"Eduardo."

Chubby grinned and nudged his inky *amigo*.

"I had a brother by that name. *Hermanos*, no?"

Hardly, Ed thought, but shared the grin with a shrug.

"Brothers help each other sometimes. *Es verⸯaⸯ?*" Chubby asked.

"Sometimes. Sure." And there it is, Ed thought. The pitch.

"You have many cameras. Cameras watching all the time."

"Yeah. Whole place is wired. High definition."

"High definition," Chubby said, except it was "high def-ee-neesh-on."

"We don't miss much."

"And you sometimes are the one to watch these cameras?"

"Sometimes." He spent an hour or more every shift in the surveillance room. Four guards on each shift rotated indoor patrol, parking lot prowls, and monitor duty.

"And you record what you are watching? You keep this video how many days?" *Vee-ⸯee-oh.*

"It's stored on a hard drive for thirty days. It's a state law." Ed thought he had heard Shift Commander Doug say that once.

"So, you could see what was happening last night?"

"Like a rerun."

"Like a rerun." Chubby let out a high titter and nudged his compadre again. The tatted-up *hombre* growled something Ed didn't catch. Chubby cleared his throat and leaned over the table to tap a finger by Ed's paper plate.

Ed took a sip of lemonade and waited for the guy to get to his point.

"We would like to see something that happened last night."

And there it was.

"Our niece has run away from home. Our sister is *muy* upset by this, you know? *Claro?* We know she came here last night to meet someone. A *boy*, maybe."

"And you want to see the footage to find out who she took off with," Ed said.

Chubby's fixed grin broadened. His *amigo* tried a smile, too. The effect was disturbing.

"That's not so easy. We're not supposed to allow anyone into the monitor room unless a formal complaint has been made."

Chubby nodded.

"But you probably have a reason you don't want to make a formal complaint."

Chubby shook his head, eyes closed and lower lip thrust out.

"But it's your niece, right? Your sister is worried."

"Very worried, *mi hermana.*"

Ed took a long pull from his lemonade. He wiped his lips with a napkin and dropped the napkin into the puddle of red grease on his plate. He waited while Chubby counted one, two, three, four, five, six fifty-dollar bills onto the table. Ed covered the bills with his plate.

"Be by the restrooms outside the security office at three," Ed directed.

"At three," Chubby agreed. Both men slid from the booth and walked away into the main mall.

Yes, best job I ever ha in my life*, Ed thought.

11

It was full-on night when the bus slowed to a stop. Levon sensed this was the end of the ride by the wakeful attitude of the men around him. He leaned from the bench to see the glare of the bus's headlights against high cyclone fencing. The front doors hissed open, and a man in a sharply pressed navy-blue uniform worn under a quilted nylon jacket stepped in with a clipboard in his hand. He took papers from the driver and checked them against his list before doing a headcount of his own.

Once he'd stepped off, the bus continued through a gate and along a winding road that led to a second gate and another headcount by another guard in blue. This guard stayed with them as they moved through the second checkpoint and between rows of buildings before coming to a stop again. Three more guards entered the bus and worked their way between the benches to free everyone from the ring bolts. Still wearing the belt manacles, they were ordered to stand and file out of the bus.

The bus rested on a gravel lot under the harsh glare

of banks of lights mounted on the roofs of single-story buildings that resembled barracks. The buildings were old, with crumbling stucco faces covered in thick coats of bright yellow paint. Barred windows were spaced along the walls. Levon could see fists gripping the bars behind the streaked glass. The men inside were curious about the new arrivals.

The clipboard guard from the bus barked, and the prisoners formed a ragged row as the empty vehicle pulled away. He strode the line, pointing at one man or another. Guards would remove the cuffs and belts and manacles from each in turn. They were given numbers and trotted off into the gloom beyond the lake of bright lights. The number of their assigned buildings, Levon guessed. Most of these guys had to be repeat offenders. They knew the drill, and where to find their new digs.

He noticed that none of the guards were armed with weapons other than the truncheons that hung from their equipment belts. The clipboard guard had a rattan rod tucked under one arm, with a leather-wrapped handle and a lanyard at the end. He was a mean-looking bastard with a long sharp nose and close-set eyes.

The sorting continued according to the scheme on the clipboard until only Levon and the three political prisoners were left. The cold air was biting, with a dampness that created a bone-deep chill. Gusts of wind blew hard enough between the buildings to rustle their clothing, and there was a tang of salt in the air. They were either on the Med or the Black Sea Coast. Levon had never heard of Tekirdağ, and so had no way of knowing. He stood at ease with his hands clasped behind him, as did the man in fatigues. The other two, the suits, stood shivering, hugging their arms around them, faces pinched and white.

Clipboard walked in front of them, eyeballing them. He showed little interest in Levon. When he came to the young man in fatigues, he stepped in closer, right inside the man's space. He was shorter than the soldier and was forced to look up at him. He craned his neck so he could sneer inches from the taller man's face. He said something to the soldier that Levon could neither hear nor understand. Flecks of spittle from Clipboard's lips made dark dots on the tan cloth of the soldier's blouse.

With a sudden movement, he thrust the corner of the clipboard into the soldier's gut, folding the man over. The clipboard in both hands, the guard brought it down hard over the back of the soldier's head, dropping him to the gravel on his knees. He spat on the soldier's back and hissed a curse.

A wave of his hand, and two guards had the soldier up and frog-walked him away into the dark between two buildings. Another gesture and the two suits were led away as well, leaving only Levon standing alone.

"English?" Clipboard asked.

"Canadian."

"Number foor-teen. You know number *foor-teen*?"

"Yes."

"You are in *foor-teen* with other *yabanci*. Euros. You know?"

"Foreigners."

Clipboard nodded to another guard, who trotted forward.

"I'd like to speak to someone from the Canadian consulate," Levon said.

With lightning speed, Clipboard struck out, this time with the rattan switch. Levon tasted salt before he felt the sting. The end of the switch had opened a strip of flesh along his jaw. The strike was hard enough to cut the flesh inside his mouth against his teeth. Don't speak unless spoken to. Noted.

Levon was led into the dark to a second row of buildings behind the ones where the bus had dropped them. His escort gestured for him to step back and keep his hands atop his head. The numeral 14 was stenciled in black on the bright yellow stucco. The guard undid locks on a wooden door, swung it open, and made a sweeping motion toward the interior. Levon stepped into the gloom, then heard the door slam shut behind him and the rattle of the lock being secured.

He stood for a moment, allowing his eyes to adjust to the minimal light coming in through the grimy glass outside the bars on the windows. He could still see his breath. He was out of the wind, but it was still cold in the building.

Someone was coughing somewhere. Someone else spat. The sound echoed off the bare walls of a high-ceilinged room. Levon sensed a confined space filled with men.

A long, narrow corridor was visible now, in shades of gray. It ran the length of the building. It was lined on either side by open doorways, and had a vaulted ceiling high above the tops of the cells, out of reach of even the tallest man standing atop a cell wall. Figures slumped in the doorways or leaned out to catch a glimpse of the new man. A solitary figure stood in the center of the corridor, a diminutive man with a tuft of hair at the crown of his head that shone whitish in the scant light. His eyes gleamed as his head turned, the glare from a doorway reflecting off his eyeglasses. He was wrapped in a blanket he wore like a serape.

"*Deutsch? Francois?* Yankee? *Zu groß, um Japaner zu sein*," the man in the blanket said.

"Canadian," Levon replied.

"*Kana•isch?* Québécois or English?" The voice was German-accented. Low German. Munich or Heidelberg.

"English."

"Well, let me show you to your room." The man in the blanket turned to move down the hallway.

Levon spat out a mouthful of blood and followed.

12

"That girl eats like she's never *seen* food before," Uncle Fern said as he finished building a third stack of pancakes. He set them down in the middle of the table in front of Esperanza. She was spooning bacon and eggs onto a wedge of buttered toast.

"Well, look at her," Merry said. "She sure hasn't seen food like this in a long time."

"Or any kind of decent bed or bath."

"She slept almost sixteen hours straight. I didn't know that was possible."

"It is when you've been tired for a long time. Or scared. Or both."

Merry looked at her plate, poking a fork into what was left of her scrambled eggs.

Fern took a seat between them in the sunny kitchen of his cabin in the woods. He poured himself a mug of coffee and sat marveling at the sheer poundage the little girl was packing away. His three hounds had circled the table a few times and made sad puppy eyes at the girl, who ignored them as if they weren't there. When it was clear she wouldn't be sharing her breakfast with them, they filed out through the doggie door, looking for something to chase. Fern Cade's other dog, a Rhodesian ridgeback, was curled up under the table at Merry's feet.

"Now, you know I didn't buy that whopper you told me last night for a minute," Fern said to Merry.

"Sorry, sir," Merry said, eyes cast down.

"A foreign exchange student staying with the Hamers. You know one phone call to Jessie is all it takes to blow that one all to hell?"

"Yes, sir."

"So, stop bullshitting your old uncle and tell me where this girl came from."

Merry laid out the timeline and described the men and how they were keeping Esperanza like a slave to steal for them. The girl looked up from eating at the mention of her name and beamed a maple-syrup-smeared smile at them both. Merry ended her story with a plea to her uncle not to tell Jessie Hamer about this.

"I'll take all the blame. Sandy didn't want to do this," Merry pleaded.

"I guess you did the right thing," Fern said.

It was his turn to lie. The old man knew damned sure his niece had done the right thing. This poor little thing eating like a termite at his table couldn't be more than twelve. The bad *hombres* playing Fagan to her Oliver Twist would surely have turned Esperanza to more profitable labor once she'd matured a bit. God only knows, they might have turned her out already or abused her themselves. Fern pushed his imagination away from what this little one's life had been like since leaving wherever she called home. Human traffickers thought of their charges as property, living cash machines. They treated them worse than livestock. He'd seen his share when he served in Southeast Asia. Children with painted faces offered up by pimps who were just as likely to be their siblings or even parents. He doubted Esperanza's story was much different. Probably bought for a price somewhere and brought across the border with someone posing as her father or mother. And he was sure Levon's daughter had spared this one from a life of hell.

"Well, she can stay here until we come up with something better," he said. "But no more lies."

"Yes, sir. No, sir."

"When you lie like that, it makes me think *you* think your old uncle is some kind of moron."

"Yes, sir. I mean, *no,* sir!" Merry said. A hand leapt to her mouth to stifle a giggle. Esperanza laughed too, looking from one to another. Not getting the joke, of course, but joining in anyway.

"We'll need some rules here. A plan of attack," Fern continued.

"What's that mean?"

"She's an illegal, Merry. I know that ain't her fault, but she's trouble for us, and here we just got ourselves *outta* trouble." And they had. Merry had only been back home for a few weeks after being placed in foster care by court order. Fern endured the near-constant presence of federal agents poking around and asking questions. For now, the revenuers had stopped coming by looking for her father. That didn't mean they might not come back.

"I'm sorry," Merry said.

"Better to apologize than ask permission sometimes. Learned that in the Corps. But we need to make sure she stays outta sight when any strangers come by.

And she can't leave the farm until we're one hundred percent no one's looking for her."

Merry nodded.

"Poor little thing," Fern said, looking at the girl, cheeks stuffed and eyes gleaming.

"Did you get anything to eat, uncle? You need me to fix you something?" Merry asked, rising to take her plate and glass to the sink.

"Coffee's fine. You gonna introduce her to your animals?"

"As soon as she's done eating and washes up. She can help me groom Bravo." Bravo was Merry's chestnut gelding.

"Make sure you warn her about Tricky Dick," Fern said. Tricky Dick was his name for the Abyssinian goat Merry kept as a barn-mate for her horse. Merry had originally named him Brewster, but even she had recently started using her uncle's sobriquet for the mischievous animal, who liked to butt anyone unwary enough to turn their back on him.

"Roger that." She returned to the table to take Esperanza's empty dishes.

Esperanza whispered a *gracias* to Fern and joined her new friend at the sink to help with the washing up. Fern listened to the pair chattering away over the sound of running water and clanking dishware. His niece spoke Spanish without hesitation, the apple not falling far from the tree. There was much of her father in the girl, even Levon's ease with languages. The pair began laughing.

"You two wouldn't be talking about me, would you?" he asked, turning his chair.

"I was just telling Esperanza she has maple syrup in her hair." Merry, giggling, held up a sticky lock of the smaller girl's long black hair.

"Maybe she'd like her hair cut," Fern said.

"*¿Te gustaría que te cortara el pelo más corto?*" Merry said, turning to her.

The smaller girl thought about this, lips pressed together, before nodding with vigor and a pearly smile.

13

"You probably think you're in for the worst week of your life," Gunny Leffertz said. "You'd be wrong."

He walked in front of a double row of men standing at ease in the center of a fenced compound, two rows of five in white t-shirts and drawstring running pants. The gunny wore pressed BDUs in digital sea camo and had an old-school campaign hat pressed down on his head. The globe-and-anchor pin on the crown was polished to a gleam. His eyes were hidden by mirrored Oakleys.

He stopped, hands clasped behind his back, and listened for a moment to the wind whispering through the pines across the broad killing zone beyond the double fence.

"Someday, you're gonna be in the shit. Deep in the real shit, up to your eyelids. Maybe you'll get your ass lost someplace where there ain't a friend in sight. Maybe you'll find yourself in the snow, or the water, or out in a desert somewhere a thousand miles from anyone who gives a shit about you and your problems. Maybe your ass will get grabbed up by some real motherfuckers, mean motherfuckers, who want to know what you know and will do anything to get you to tell them."

The boughs of the trees shush-shushed.

"Anything!"

The gunny shouted it. Three of the men flinched at the sudden sound. Gunny heard their sneakered feet shift in the sand. He turned his back to them to hide the thin smile that creased his lips. Damn, he loved his work.

"And that will be the worst week of your life. And you will look back on your days here with me as a vacation. A fucking time-out from the cares and worries of the sheer hell you might face one day. This will be your spring break. You will thank Jesus for the time you spent here. And do you know why that is?"

None of the men answered. The gunny had not addressed any of them individually. He turned back to face them.

"Because this is where you will learn how to get your ass through the worst time of your life. I will test you. I will hurt you. You will be hot. You will be cold. You will be hungry. Hell, I'm gonna try to drown you. You might even think I'm trying to kill you. But I'm not."

He stepped up closer, standing directly before a tall white boy.

"I am gonna temper you. I am gonna forge you. And if you break here, then you will break downrange. I will find your weaknesses. I will find what scares you. I will hammer away at you, sleeping and waking."

The white boy's face betrayed nothing. His gaze remained fixed on the tops of the swaying pines beyond the wire.

"And you will walk away from here a man. Or you will be carried out of here a broke-ass, useless, weak-kneed pussy. How are you leaving here, boy?"

He had been addressed directly, so the white boy answered.

"Walking, Gunny."

Gunny stepped within inches of the white boy. He wrinkled his nose, taking a few deep sniffs.

"You smell like trouble, son. Are you gonna make trouble for me?"

"Yes, Gunny."

Gunny removed his Oakleys. His eyes had a cast over them beneath scarred lids that hung heavy. He locked the white boy with his blind, unblinking stare.

"You been in trouble, boy?"

"A time or two, Gunny."

"Been inside, right?"

"Six months in county, Gunny. Stole a few cars, Gunny."

"You ever try to escape?"

"Yes, Gunny."

"Ever make it?"

"Got out for a week, Gunny. Earned me another month, Gunny."

"Where you from? Alabama? Florida Panhandle?"

"Alabama, Gunny."

"Are you a redneck? Or are you a hillbilly?"

"A hillbilly, Gunny."

Gunny snorted and stepped back. He replaced his Oakleys over his sightless eyes.

"What branch of the United States military took a squat and shat you onto me, son?"

"The Marine Corps, Gunny."

"How my Corps has fallen prey to the times, allowing

a pogue like you to wear the globe and anchor. You have a name, pogue?"

"Levon Cade, Gunny."

"Cade, I'm gonna enjoy breaking your hillbilly ass, you car-thieving, sister-fucking, nigger-hating son of a bitch."

"Yes, Gunny."

14

Gunny Leffertz said:
*"Details. Details. Details. Take it all in. You never
know what might turn out to be important."*

The morning call to prayer echoed through the camp
from a loudspeaker set atop the admin building.

Levon woke, stretched, and began running in place
in the cell he shared with six other men. He needed
to limber up the muscles that ached from a cold night
on the cement floor. Running restored circulation and
brought his legs and arms back to life. His stomach
rumbled. No food since sometime the day before.

He needed to eat. He needed a coat. He needed a
blanket and a bunk. He needed a phone. In that order.

The cell was built for two but housed six. Two men
shared one bunk, a heavy-set Belgian and a lazy looking
Thai with large eyes and the body of a boy. The second
bunk belonged to a surly Corsican with a boxer's build
and a weepy eye turned milky-white with a cataract.
Levon shared the floor with his German friend from
the night before and a middle-aged Japanese man

wearing a pair of horn-rim eyeglasses repaired with wire.

The others watched Levon's exercise routine. Any kind of distraction was welcome. Other men gathered at the open cell door, smoking and exchanging remarks in a peculiar patois of combined languages. The demographics leaned to European, with a few Asians and Africans. No Turks, Arabs, Kurds, or Uzbeks here. This was the infidel wing of the prison.

He stopped running in place when he started to pop a sweat. Vapor rose from his head in the frigid air.

"You are a soldier, yes?" the fat Belgian asked, first in French, then in Dutch. Levon pretended not to understand.

"He wants to know if you are a soldier," the German said.

"I'm an aid worker," Levon told them.

For some reason, that provoked a laugh from a few of the men.

"When do we eat?" Levon asked the German.

"When they call our hut number," the German said and stuck his hand out. "Klaus."

"Bill Hogue," Levon said and took the smaller man's hand.

* * *

"*On ˌört! On ˌört!*" A call came from outside as the locks were undone on the barracks door. Fourteen. The number of Levon's new home.

Levon joined a loose column of men moving toward the far end of the camp and a low wooden building. Smoke dropped from a metal pipe atop the roof to drift away in a fog and gather in the lane between the buildings. A scent heavy with garlic and grilled meat rode the haze. Levon's stomach clenched.

It was cold and overcast, and a wind from the out-of-sight sea somewhere beyond the evergreen woods carried a chilling mist with it. Every surface was covered in a cold coat of salt slick.

Despite his need for food, he dawdled a bit, falling back in the column for a good look around his new environs—three rows of five barracks buildings on a gravel lot with the cookhouse and a two-story administration building or guard shack at one end. The admin building was a sheet-steel structure and the newest construction in the yard. It was enclosed by its own fence topped with razor wire, which had a gateway equipped with a keypad. It was large enough to house the number of guards he'd seen so far. That meant they were paramilitary, housed here with the convicts 24/7. At the opposite end of the broad gravel lane was a low, windowless building painted the same bright yellow as the barracks. Showers and latrine, probably.

The buildings sat at the center of a broad pasture of mown grass that was surrounded on all sides by a high fence with hoops of razor wire run in triple rows. Six watchtowers stood on the outside of the interior row of fencing with a second, exterior row forming a corridor that ran all the way around the camp. Four of the towers were concrete construction. The remaining two were girders topped with a wooden box. He doubted they were all occupied, but could see the reflection of protective domes that sheltered their cameras from the elements. There were cameras under the eaves of some of the barracks buildings as well.

Bundles of wires ran from the towers and were draped along the fence tops and slung over the corridor to terminate at the guard shack. There'd be a surveillance room in there. He'd have to find a way in there to map out whatever blind spots there might be.

He'd dropped to the back of the column. A guard growled at him, and Levon joined the other men gathered in a tight row to enter the dining hall.

It was warmer inside. Sufi music played on the tinny speakers of a radio. The scent of cooked meat and spices overwhelmed even the odor coming off the clutch of men waiting their turn at a steam counter that ran across the rear of the space. Some men were already seated at the long picnic-type steel tables, eating from trays.

Levon took a plastic tray from a stack at the head of the serving line. It was indented to receive portions of food. There were cigarette burns in it. He took a short-tined plastic fork and a spoon from a rubber bus tub.

A fat Turk in an apron worn over a t-shirt supervised other men dishing out portions from a row of steel trays. He wore a hair net that covered his balding head but not his arms, which were furred like an ape's. A spoonful of greasy rice. Another of greasy beans. A clump of stringy lamb that added to the pool of grease. At the end of the steam table were platters piled with squares of white and black bread. Levon took one of each, and the hairy chef's shout, along with the narrowed eyes of the men behind him, made him return one of the squares to its place. One to a customer.

He took his tray to sit across the table from the German, with the Japanese man from their cell beside him. Only the rice and beans remained on their trays. The Belgian sat at the far end of their table, his tray heaped with a triple portion of lamb and three squares of bread. He shared them with the little Thai seated close beside him.

The radio switched to Egyptian pop music. Levon dug into the mess on his plate.

"I need a blanket and a coat. Where did you get yours?" Levon asked after he'd downed the bulk of his meal.

"And *guten morgen* to you, *mein freun*," Klaus said, but he was smiling.

"I need to get stuff."

"Then you will need money. Do you have money?" Klaus asked.

"They took it all."

"Then no blanket and no coat." The Japanese spoke for the first time.

"Gedde is right. Money talks here. Or cigarettes. Or dope." Klaus shrugged.

"Where do you get your money?" Levon asked them.

"I have friends outside," Klaus said. Gedde said nothing.

"I've been denied contact."

"A political prisoner?" Klaus asked.

"I guess. I don't know."

Klaus said nothing. It was clear from his half-lidded eyes that he was assessing Levon.

"You are a liar, but who in here is not? You will not last long. It will be colder next month, and colder still the month after."

"Is there a way to earn money here?" Levon said.

"Yes. *Natürlich*. But you do not look like a man who would do the work required," Klaus said. Gedde blinked, awaiting Levon's reply.

"Like what?" Levon said.

"Be someone's woman. Like the *Belgier's* little toy boy," Klaus said. Gedde's eyes cut to the fat man dropping morsels of bread onto the tongue of the Thai, his mouth open in imitation of a baby bird in a nest.

"There has to be other work in a place like this." Levon mopped the last of the grease from his tray with a square of bread.

"There is always murder," Klaus suggested.

"You said I don't look like a man who would do that."

"I also said we are all liars."

"Who hires for that kind of work?"

"The Chechen."

"He have a name?"

"Only 'The Chechen.'"

"Can you point him out to me, Klaus?"

"I could, but I will not. I think it is wisest that you and I not be friends, Canadian Bill."

"I'll find him on my own, then." Levon rose to take his tray and utensils and dump them into one of the trashcans filled with soapy water that stood by the door to the yard.

"You will not help him?" Gedde asked.

"And neither will you. Not if you ever want to see Osaka again," Klaus said and removed his tray from the table.

15

It was far too important a decision to be made by Merry and Esperanza alone.

So Sandy Hamer drove over with an armload of magazines. After two hours in Merry's room, a choice was made.

"This," Esperanza said. She held up a magazine showing Natalie Portman with a blunt cut that just touched her shoulders.

"It's cute!" Sandy proclaimed.

"You're sure?" Merry asked.

Esperanza nodded.

They gathered scissors, brushes, combs, and a can of mousse borrowed from Sandy's mom. Newspapers were laid down, and a kitchen chair set in place atop them. The instruments were placed on a towel on the dresser.

"Do you think we can do this?" Sandy asked.

"It looks simple enough. It's just hair," Merry told her.

"But look at it. All the way down her back. I bet it's never been cut!"

"It's not like we can take her to Super Cuts, okay?"

Esperanza sat upright in the chair, wide eyes glancing from one girl to another. Merry offered soothing words and began brushing the thick black mane.

"God, I wish I was that skinny!" Sandy moaned.

"She's not skinny, Sands. She's malnourished."

"Lucky girl."

"Hold up the magazine."

Esperanza held statue-still as Merry finished brushing her hair smooth and gathered it behind her head. The girl was already looking better after only two days at the Cade farm. The dark circles under her eyes were nearly gone. Two nights of sound sleep and three meals a day had taken the gaunt, drawn look from her features. Her face was regaining the heart-shape of a pretty young girl.

All the more pressure on Merry not to screw up her first haircut.

"Here goes," Merry said.

After few false starts, whispered consultations, and a carpet of fine black hair spread around the chair, Merry had accomplished a near-approximation of the actress's cut. She and Sandy held their breath when Esperanza leapt up to run into the bathroom for her first look in the mirror. The girl returned, a smile stretching her cheeks and tears in her eyes. She gripped Merry in a tight hug.

"I guess she likes it," Sandy said.

* * *

A commercial van was parked on the asphalt circle ringing the old live oak that shaded Jessie Hamer's house. It was a real shitbox, with primer spots and faded sections on the sides where the company logo had been peeled away or scraped off. Blue vapor fell from the exhaust pipe. Someone inside was running the heater to stay warm.

Jessie eyed the van as she rolled past to where she usually parked her work truck in its space in front of the barn. Her truck bore the logo for Riverstone Veterinary, featuring a silhouette of a dressage horse.

If she disliked the van, she liked the occupants even less. A man exited the van either side to walk over and meet her between the barn and house. The pair, a heavy man in a woolen jacket and a leaner one in a hoodie and windbreaker, stood on either side of the crushed stone walkway that led to the house. The heavy guy smiled under tinted aviators. The younger man looked like he'd rather be back in the van napping.

"Excuse me, miss. I am looking for my daughter," the heavy man said.

"Here?" Jessie said. She stopped on the walk, hands deep in the pockets of her sheep-shearing barn coat. Five paces between her and the men. Not far enough. Levon had told her about the ten-paces rule, but she recalled it too late. He also told her to always heed that little whispering voice. He said it was their Neanderthal ancestors deep down in our shared psyche offering a warning across the eons. The voice was deafening now. These men were *all* wrong.

"Not here. But someone here might know where she is," the man said.

"Really." Not a question.

The man reached into a pocket of his coat. Jessie's hand tightened on the pritchel she held in her pocket. It was a slender forged-steel spike used to punch nail holes into horseshoes, a farrier's tool that she was fully ready to plunge into the man's smiling face if he stepped too close.

Tesoro stayed where he was, sensing her reticence, understanding that there was a gulf between them he could not cross. They were off to a bad start, and there was no going back to being friendly strangers. The woman made no effort to hide her suspicion or defiance. She was gripping something deep in her coat pocket. It could very well be a gun, and she could very well be good with it. He and Buey would back off for now, and play it cool.

"My daughter, you see. She run away from home. We think someone here might have seen her."

"Where's home?"

"¿Que?"

"You said she ran away from home. Where is home?"

Tesoro blinked before answering, "Chattanooga." *Shat-ah-new•ge-uh.*

"Uh-huh. So why do you think your daughter is here?"

Tesoro unfolded a piece of paper and held it out to her. A photograph of some kind.

"This car. The license plate. It is a car from this place, this address."

The Kia. The car she let Sandy drive.

"I haven't seen your daughter."

"Maybe it was not you driving. This is Huntsville. At a mall. This is my daughter getting into this car."

What the hell did you do, Sandy?

"The car's not here right now," she said.

"I see that. Where is it?"

Jessie realized they had probably already looked for it before she arrived. How long had they been waiting for someone to come home?

"It's at a garage in Haley. It's been there all week. Transmission trouble."

The heavy man did not acknowledge her answer. He kept her fixed in his gaze through the tinted lenses. The other man turned his head to look around, weighing a decision, making an assessment. Jessie leaned back on her right foot, her mind racing. Fight or flight. Where to land on that question? She knew, in the end, it was her body, not her mind, that would make that choice.

"I think someone borrow your car. Take it for a ride. *Claro?*" The heavy man's smile returned.

"That must be what happened."

"*Sí.* Yes. We go now. Thank you for your time."

Jessie offered no reply.

He grunted something to the younger man, and both of them backed away before returning to their van. The van ground into gear and drove around the circle and down the driveway toward the county road.

Jessie walked to the house, conscious that they would be watching her as they pulled away. Because of that, she fought down the urge to run into the house for the telephone.

16

The gravel gave way to rough grass at the back of the camp. A football pitch was set up, its goals draped with sagging nets at either end.

Levon joined men walking out to either watch or play. A few men were stripped to their shorts to kick and head a ball around while waiting for enough players to start a game. Some took up seats on benches made from wood planks and stacked bricks. Others stood in clutches smoking and talking. The sickly-sweet tang of hashish joined the smell of tobacco smoke. A pair of indifferent guards watched from a corner of the field. There were rules and there were rules, and they were applied with discretion here.

Arabs and Turks eyeballed Levon but did not approach or address him directly. He regarded them as well, sizing up the quilted denim jackets a few of them wore. Most had keffiyehs secured around their necks against the cold breeze coming through the fence. Levon stood watching, hands in his armpits.

There were enough men on the field now for sides, but still the game did not start, just squats and stretches and grab-ass. A few ran around doing practice kicks. Levon noticed the ball for the first time, weakly inflated and patched with duct tape. Its once-colorful skin was faded and scuffed.

Some of the conversations stopped. The men on the benches turned their heads. The teams stood looking back toward the barracks. Levon turned to see a trio of men coming toward them. Most noticeable was a man in a white fedora, wearing a North Face parka in bright red. Walking to one side of him was a smaller man carrying a net sack filled with balls. To the other side of the fedora was a man as tall as Levon, but even broader across the chest and shoulders, and he had a thick neck as wide across as his too-small head. His shaved scalp exaggerated the effect. This man carried a folded lawn chair.

The players trotted to the edge of the field to accept the sack of balls. All looked new, bright, and free of patches. The big man unfolded the lawn chair and took great care to make sure it was secure and level at the edge of the pitch. The fedora settled into the chair, and the ball boy lit the end of a black cigar for him. He then removed a thermos from a pocket inside his coat and poured a cup of something steaming that the fedora took without acknowledgment. The ball boy set the thermos down before taking a seat on the grass like a dog might by its master. The big guy with the little head remained standing, huge arms crossed and eyes dull. The fedora waved a hand, and the game began. Half the men on the field stripped down to bare chests, and the play was on.

Levon waited until the break at half-time to make his approach. He stopped far enough away so as not to pose a threat, but close enough to be heard. The muscle with the small head tensed and locked Levon in a death stare.

"I am looking for work," Levon said in Russian.

The Chechen took a mouthful of cigar smoke and glanced at Levon from under the brim of his fedora. In his own language, he spoke to the ball boy, who snickered.

"I am not a Russian," Levon said.

The Chechen tipped the brim of hat back to give Levon a fresh appraisal.

"I see you have met *ₑlora borsza.*" He pointed the cigar at the scabbed-over gash on Levon's jaw. He'd switched to Russian. *Dlora borsza* loosely translated to "that prick" in Chechen.

"Do you have work for me?" Levon asked.

"You are not that pretty." That made the ball boy giggle.

"You know the kind of work I mean."

"Let me see your hands."

Levon stepped closer, holding his hands out to the Chechen.

"Those are good hands. Those are hands for a certain brand of work."

"I want a blanket. A coat and a phone."

"You do not want a bed?"

"I can get that on my own."

The Chechen snapped the brim of his fedora back in place. He blew a stream of creamy smoke at the back of his own hand. He took a sip of tea.

"I have a man for that kind of work," he said finally.

Levon took two steps closer and drove his flexed hand deep into the broad throat of the man with a too-small head. The big man expelled a fine mist of blood-flecked spittle and made to step away, but Levon had him by the ears. The American used this double grip to yank the big man's face down to meet his rising knee, which cannoned into the big man's face. A wet crunch and the big man dropped to the grass, hands twitching. His nose was smeared across his face in a bloody mass of torn flesh. His dumb eyes stared up sightlessly.

"You could do better," Levon said.

Ball Boy leapt to his feet, a hand snaking beneath his coat. The Chechen waved him away.

"Are you dead, Yuri?" the Chechen asked. He poked a toe at the big man.

The big man answered with a keening, bubbling moan.

"Looks to me like you have an opening," Levon said.

"I will get you a blanket and a coat. A phone must wait until you've earned it."

"When do I start?"

"When I give you a name."

Levon nodded once and turned to go. The lawn chair creaked as the Chechen spoke after him.

"What is *your* name?"

"Bill Hogue."

"Do not do anything like that again without my permission, Beel." The chair creaked again as game play began.

Levon returned to the barracks area. The two guards at the edge of the pitch watched him until he was out of sight.

17

Jessie opened the liquor cabinet in the den for the first time in seven years. Since the day a nervous Army Reserve lieutenant was sent over from Anniston to tell her Gary wasn't coming home from Iraq. The layer of dust atop the cabinet was evidence that she stayed out of this room. The only dust-free object in the room was the framed shadowbox that hung over the bar. It held Gary's commendations and his master sergeant's stripes. Sandy must come in here and wipe it down now and then. Funny that Jessie never noticed that before.

She blew the dust from a tumbler and poured herself three fingers of Dewar's before taking the phone from her pocket. How to play this? What would she say to Sandy? What questions would she ask her daughter, and would she learn the truth?

Her questions answered versus her child's safety. Whatever else happened, she wanted that Kia kept as far from this house as possible for as long as possible. That cleared things up as far as priorities went. She tapped Sandy's picture on the screen. The glass was empty, but she didn't remember drinking it. The smoky taste on her tongue confirmed that she had. Disgusting. Scotch tasted better with a cigarette, but she'd left both habits far behind her.

"Mom?" Sandy's voice was fresh from laughing.

"Hey, honey." Jessie kept her tone light, she hoped. "Tell you what, you think you could stay at Merry's tonight?"

"I'm sure it would be okay. Why?" There was the noise of a television in the background. Music and voices. Girls talking.

"Oh, the water heater busted. No hot water until I can get a plumber out here."

"Ooh. Sure. I'll run over and get some clothes, and—"

"No! You don't want to come back here. There's water everywhere. The hall carpet and your bedroom are soaking."

"Oh."

"It's gonna take me most of the evening to wet-vac it up."

"Maybe I should come back and help?" Her dear daughter was offering her services as a question. Jessie gave her the answer she was praying for.

"You stay. I can manage. It's just a pain in the ass, is all."

"Okay. All right. You sure you're gonna be okay?"

"Yes, honey. Thanks for offering. You and Merry have a good time. Love you."

"Love you." The call ended on Sandy's end.

That was tonight. But what about tomorrow, and all the days after that? Those two men wouldn't give up. She knew her visceral reaction to them had been correct. They were bad news, and it had nothing to do with them being Hispanic. Not unusual to see Mexicans in the county, but not this time of year. Plenty of farms hired migrants during the growing and harvesting seasons. Some of the horse farms she did work for hired workers, probably illegals, to load hay and put up fencing. There was enough of a transient population around that even the few businesses in Colby had bilingual signs.

No, it was an aura or something in the way the pair moved. Especially the younger one. His constantly searching predator eyes belied his air of studied indifference. The heavier, older man wore a smile that hid an air of threat, of dire consequences if he were to encounter any kind of disappointment. The story about his daughter was pure bullshit. He didn't start by asking Jessie if he'd seen her little girl. He didn't offer to show Jessie a picture. It was the car, the Kia, that interested him.

And that van. It was creepy as shit. A rolling horror movie.

Jessie sat down on one of the padded stools at the bar with the phone still in her hand. She debated calling the police but was reluctant to do so. Blame mountain pride. Blame her mulish stubborn streak. But the Cades had had more than their share of trouble with the law, and she was not about to allow that camel to stick its nose in their tent again. Not without a lot more cause.

The car, and Sandy, were safe for the night, parked way up a lonely holler at Fern Cade's farm. They were all safe from the two *amigos* for tonight.

Her daughter, Merry Cade, and that third girl she had heard speaking Spanish between snorts of laughter.

18

"I'm gonna have to charge you deer-season rates," Lonnie Childs said from behind the counter at the Hill 'n' Dale Motel.

"What other rate is there?" Tesoro asked.

"Well, April to October, we rent to Mexicans. Rooms by the month for planters, packers, and pickers. Cheaper rate, y'know? But come November it's all deer hunters, and they pay more, and by the night."

"We are hunters," Tesoro said.

Buey hissed through his teeth at that from where he lounged on a sagging sofa, leafing through an ancient copy of *Hoy!* he found on a stack of magazines piled on a chipped coffee table.

"Oh, sorry. No offense. Didn't mean to assume," Lonnie said.

"*De na‹a.*"

"Sure, sure. A double, okay? Two full-sized beds."

"Yes. We will take that."

"Hundred for the night. Five hundred for the week."

"We will take the week." Tesoro thumbed bills from a roll onto the counter.

"Cash. Okay. Sure. Cash is king."

Lonnie put aside the clipboard with forms that the state required for occupancy and scooped up the fifties and hundreds. He got the pair of *amigos* their key and wished them a good night. They exited to move their van down to a space in front of their room, farther along the L-shaped single-story structure.

As he slipped the bills under the cash tray and closed the drawer, he realized he hadn't asked them what they hunted.

* * *

They were, in fact, cousins, not *amigos*.

Tesoro lay back atop the stiff covers of the bed nearest the window, smoking and tabbing the TV remote until he found a woman with big tits reading the news on Univision.

Buey had stripped to his tighty-whities and was halfway through his twice-a-day regimen of one hundred push-ups.

"You make me tired." Tesoro sighed.

"It was the only good habit I picked up in prison," Buey said, back rising and falling between the beds.

"You are not in prison now, *ese*."

"I have to stay hard in case I ever go back."

Tesoro pursed his lips and blew twin streams of smoke from his nostrils. It was a conversation they'd had many times before. It served as an entrée to more immediate concerns. Buey leapt to his feet to roll atop the second bed, chest and arms shiny with fresh sweat. He lay back, resting his head on folded arms. Tesoro flipped channels until he found a show with a grown man dressed only in a diaper and baby bonnet waving an out-sized rattle. The audience was howling, but

to Tesoro, it looked stupid. He was about to switch
channels when a big-breasted redhead in a tight baby-
doll outfit curvetting onto the screen.

"What is the plan here, *vato?*" Buey asked.

"We find the car. We find the girl."

"The mother. She was lying. I know."

"The car will be impossible to find in these
mountains."

"Umm." Tesoro nodded in agreement.

Both he and Buey had grown up in Sinaloa, a folded
land of canyons much like the hollers here in Alabama.
The trees were different, but the land was the same.
They knew that people and things could vanish in
country like this, never to be seen again. Their first job
with the family had been digging graves in the cholla-
choked hillsides back home. They graduated, through
achievement and attrition, to join their uncle's plaza
here in the USA.

"So how we find the girl?" Buey asked. He'd bounced
off the bed and was running a towel over his arms and
legs.

"The car. The girl is with the car." Tesoro's eyes
danced as the woman on the screen bent to show
much of her bare ass as she spanked the overgrown
baby with a paddle.

"How do we find the car?"

"We watch the house. The woman's house. The car
will come back."

"And if it does not come back?"

"We will have to call *Tio* Honesto."

"He will not be happy," Buey said and entered the
bathroom to start the shower.

"I know."

Tesoro considered this with profound concern.

Their uncle's happiness was paramount, far more important to them than their own happiness. Or comfort. Or futures.

"He paid two thousand for that girl," Buey called through the open bathroom door over the sound of the shower.

"I know."

"Dollars."

"I know. I know this."

"She has only begun to repay him."

"This also, I know."

In addition to the two thousand American Honesto gave to the girl's parents, there was the expense of transporting her from Guatemala to the border crossing, then into Texas and along and along until she reached Huntsville. Every step of the way was a *cabron* with his hand out. A twenty here, a hundred pesos there. The girl had only just started working for them and had barely earned back any of the costs of bringing her here. Weigh that deficit against the girl's future potential when she was a few years older and working in a *bur*.*el,* and the loss was in the hundreds of thousands. And Tesoro and Buey knew that their uncle would do that math to the last centavo.

"So, what do we do?" Buey called.

"We find the car."

19

The clouds parted, allowing the sun to shine on the camp.

Levon stood on a patch of grass in back of the shower building to soak in the sun. His face was to the sky, eyes closed. Someone was crossing the grass behind him. He turned, hands fisted.

"I come in peace," Klaus said, hands open before him.

Levon turned back to the sun. The German joined him, lighting a cigarette and taking a long pull. The scent of the smoke was strong.

"You had a nice talk?" he asked.

"You saw?" Levon said.

"Everyone saw."

"I thought you didn't want to associate with me."

"*Was kann ich sagen?* There is no television here, and I have read all my books. Twice."

"They have books in German here?"

"I had a friend outside sending me reading material and cigarettes."

"You had a falling out?"

"I have not heard from her, so I am left to smoke this Turkish *kacke* and seek my entertainment by speaking to you."

Levon said nothing, eyes still closed and face still to the sun.

"You do not have a story to tell?" Klaus asked.

"Nothing very interesting has ever happened to me," Levon said.

"*Now* who is the liar?"

Levon basked.

"Then I will tell you my story, if only to pass the time, *ja*?"

"Go crazy, *mein freun•*," Levon said.

Klaus took another long drag.

"You have heard of phishing? Emails sent to unwary recipients asking for money or perhaps credit card numbers?"

"I don't do a lot of internet," Levon told him.

"Well, someone hacked my email account and sent pleas to everyone on my list. They claimed to be me, and said I was traveling in Turkey and had run into trouble with the police. They said my wallet and passport had been stolen, and I could not pay my hotel bill, and so was being held prisoner in my own room. The sad truth was, I actually *was* in Turkey at the time. I was running a little export scheme out of a travel agency in Izmir. Well, my mother receives this email in her inbox and panics a bit. She panics a *lot*. Her poor boy was in trouble. But rather than send money to the phishers, she calls the German embassy in Istanbul and the consulate in Izmar, and even the Turkish embassy in Berlin. She raises the hell all over the place. I guess she loves me that much, yes? In the end, the Turkish police make it their mission to find me, and I am not in a hotel in Ankara. I am in my travel agency in Izmar, where I was preparing lovely chalk replicas of the Cathedral of Sofia as gifts for my clients. However, they are only about seventy-five percent chalk; the rest is uncut Afghan white. And the police arrive at a most unfortunate time in the process. And so, because of a mother's love, I am here."

Levon smiled, then hissed a suppressed laugh through his teeth.

"So, you find this tragedy humorous? My misfortune? Perhaps you are part German, my friend," said Klaus. He said it through a smile.

"Your outside contact sending you goodies is your mom."

"She felt bad at first for causing my arrest, but over time, she decided it was all my fault in the first place."

"No books. No cigarettes."

"And none of the chocolate biscuits I like. Sad to say, even a mother's love has its limits. Do you find this so?"

"I didn't get a chance to know my mom," Levon said. Clouds scudded west to hide the sun. He rebuttoned his shirt and turned back toward the barracks. Klaus walked with him down the broad avenue where other men walked in groups of two and three.

Ball Boy, the Chechen's man, crossed the gravel toward them. He had a folded bundle in his arms that he handed to Levon before walking away.

A denim coat with a quilted felt lining and a fresh blood stain on the breast. It was the coat of the big man Levon had brought down at the football pitch. Under it was a woolen blanket with red and blue stripes. Levon slid his arms into the sleeves of the coat. The fit was good. Klaus handed back the blanket. From its folds, a piece of paper fell to the gravel. Levon picked it up.

Ka⬤ir Tiryaki

11

"A name and a hut number," Klaus said.

"You know this guy?"

"We don't mingle with the Turks. We're unclean infidels, remember?"

"A common name."

"Eleven is an isolation custody hut, Bill."

"What's that mean?"

"They house special cases there. Guys who broke the rules. There's a Greek in there who walked in front of the line at evening prayer."

"What other kinds of guys?"

"*Kin⬤erschän⬤er.* Rapists. Turks aren't like Arabs. That *scheisse* is not okay with them."

"What would the Chechen have against this one?" Levon held the paper up to Klaus. The German's eyes widened.

"I think I do not need to know how this book ends." Klaus walked away between two huts.

20

They made chocolate chip and walnut cookies, burning half of them. They watched *The Bachelor* and an *X-Men* movie before Uncle Fern chased them upstairs so he could have the TV back. Up in Merry's room, they lay in the dark talking. Esperanza had the bed, while Merry and Sandy camped out in sleeping bags on the floor. Moonlight came in through the sheers, casting the room in silver.

Merry was asking Esperanza questions and translating the answers for Sandy.

Her father worked in the oil fields while she and her mother, her grandmother, and her siblings lived in a company-owned village.

"Papa drove a truck. He hauled pipe and dug trenches. He had no skills. The pay was low. Then he got sick and could not work so hard."

"What did you do then?" Merry asked.

"We moved to Jalapa. It is nearer the capital. My father and mother and older sister got work at the *maquila•oras*."

"What's that?"

"A place of work where things are made. There are many machines there."

"Like a factory?"

"*Sí*. A factory. But it is expensive in a city like Jalapa. In the country, it is cheap to live. In the city, everything costs too high. And to get a job at the factory, you must pay the gangs. If you do not pay them, they will hurt you so you cannot work. My mama and papa and *hermana* work very hard but make little money. Not enough for my little brothers and sister to live."

"Oh, my God," Sandy exclaimed. "They *sol♦* her!"

"Shut up, Sandy," Merry said.

"My sister married a man at the factory, a *jefe*. He is a *Coreano*."

"Hold on," Merry said. "Corry-ano? He's a mailman?"

Esperanza whooped with laughter.

"What did I miss?" Sandy asked.

"He is a *coreano*. Like a *Chino* or a *Japonés*."

"You mean he's Korean?"

"*¡Sí! ¡Sí!* Koh-ree-ann! He works at the factory. It is owned by the koh-ree-anns."

"He has money?"

"*Sí*. My sister moved away with him. We never see her again. I am very happy for her but sad for me."

"And your family was still poor."

"Yes. No money from my sister. My father was still very sick and lost his job."

Esperanza told of how she woke up one night to her mother crying. Her father came to the room she shared with her brothers and sisters with a shopping bag of her clothes. He walked her from the apartment where they lived into an alley that ran behind the stores that lined a square near the factory. He knocked and a woman answered, a woman with a cruel face who took her past a room where men smoked and played cards. Esperanza looked back. The door to the alley stood open. Her father was no longer there.

The next day, the woman took her on a bus that drove north for days to a place in the north where there were many, many people living in shacks and tents. It was there she was given over to a man with a Pancho Villa mustache and a big white cowboy hat. He put her and four other girls into the back of a truck and drove them north through the night and across the border into Mexico. She didn't know this until she was told the following day on another bus traveling north. This one was filled with men and women from Guatemala and El Salvador and Honduras. A few were sick, with racking coughs or yellow skin. Some of the men were actually boys, not much older than her. They scared her with their black tattoos and shaved heads. They said things to her she could not repeat but could never forget.

Esperanza lost track of how many days she rode buses and trains and walked on roads northward as part of one group or another, always overseen by one Mexican or another who helped them with water and food along the way. After many, many days, they came to a river. They told Esperanza that the USA was on the other side, her new home. They told her how lucky she was to be going there. She did not feel lucky. She felt alone. Lost. Always frightened.

She was taken over the river on a raft of plastic drums and wooden planks. Once on the other side, she joined a column of people walking across the desert to a road where trucks waited for them. More trucks and vans and cars. More sleeping while moving. More meals that were cold and greasy and never enough.

She knew they were taking her north since the nights, and then the days, got colder. For the last leg of her journey, she traveled with four other girls a few years older than her. They were dropped off at what looked like an apartment building. She sat alone in the back of the truck for an hour's drive on a highway and a short trip along a surface road. Days riding blind had taught her the difference.

It was in an empty parking lot near railroad tracks that she was handed over to the two men Merry and Sandy saw at the mall. They taught her what to steal and how to steal it. She was good at reading, so it was easy for her to recognize the stores and the brands they wanted. They gave her special bags lined with shiny foil. They said it was magic to keep the machines from knowing that she was stealing. She knew it was science, although she did not know how it worked.

She thought she had been stealing for them for a week and a couple of days when Merry took her away. This last was spoken through tears.

"Was she raped?" Sandy asked.

"I'm not going to ask her that," Merry said.

Esperanza wanted to know what they were saying.

"Sandy wants to know if she can have those American Eagle jeans you stole," Merry said, her eyes narrowed at Sandy with shoulders raised, head tilted, and mouth slack in a "duh" gesture.

"I prayed and prayed, and Jesus saved me. He sent *you*, Merry. *Gracias, mi amiga.*" Esperanza's voice was moist with tears.

"Would you like us to pray with you?" Merry asked. "*Si.*"

They prayed together, Sandy in English, then fell silent and finally to sleep.

21

Gunny Leffertz said:
"It's the man, not the weapon."

The midday meal was stale flatbread, cheese, and a mash of peas laced heavily with garlic. Levon made a burrito and took up a place against the wall of a hut to watch the building numbered 11.

That hut remained locked until all the other men had been called to lunch. Guards, led by Clipboard, aka the Prick, came to unlock the door and escort the thirty or so men inside to the dining hall. Levon studied them, committing them to memory. Most were dark-skinned, except for a beefy Euro with a shaved scalp and a heavy ginger beard. They didn't look in either direction, only straight ahead, with the guards flanking them all the way to the chow line.

Someone called in Arabic, "*Murta•!*" Apostate. Someone, or all of them, had turned their back on Allah.

The Prick stopped in his march to look along the lane for the shouter. No one met his gaze. Levon backed farther into the shadows between the two huts. The Prick slapped his rattan flail against his leg once and rejoined the parade of pariahs now entering the dining hall.

There was a crunch of gravel behind Levon. It was the ball boy. He spoke in Turkish to Levon, who shook his head. They tried a few more languages and finally settled on French. Ball Boy's French was worse than Levon's.

"You not kill," Ball Boy said, nodding toward the dining hall.

"I do not know what he looks like, this Kadir Tiryaki."

"Is Turk. Has *tavşan ⋅u⋅ak*. It is…" Busboy brushed his fingers down his upper lip in a chopping motion.

"*Le bec-⋅e-lièvre?* A harelip?"

"Air-leep. Yes. Like the *tavşan*." Rabbit.

"Height? How tall?"

Ball Boy held his hand flat at Levon's shoulder.

"Beard? Mustache?" Levon gestured to indicate facial hair. Ball Boy tilted his chin and clicked his tongue. Turk body language for the negative.

"He wear *ceket*. Red. *Türkiye* football team. You know?"

Levon searched his memory of the column of men who had exited hut 11. There had been a man in a red team jacket. Cleanshaven. He hadn't seen the man's face clearly.

"What did he do?" Levon said.

Ball Boy blinked at him, uncomprehending.

"Why does your boss want him dead?"

"What matters? Dead is dead. You do."

"I need to know the reason. I am not your idiot friend."

"*Zampara* not my friend. You hurt. Me happy enough." Ball Boy spat.

Zampara. Levon knew that one. Motherfucker. Insults and profanity were the richest chapter in his foreign language lexicon.

"What did Tiryaki do?"

"He kill woman. Woman *chef* does not want dead."

"His wife? A relative?"

Ball Boy's face turned sour.

"A whore. She make *chef* much money. The pig kill her with hammer."

Levon searched Ball Boy's face. The contempt in the man's eyes was real, no guile there. The target was a woman-killer.

"I will do it. Tonight. Tomorrow. First opportunity."

"You need *bıçak*?" Ball Boy made a motion with his fingers joined. A blade.

"No."

The call to afternoon prayer sounded tinnily from the speaker on the admin building's roof. Ball Boy nodded once and turned away. Levon stayed to watch the men of Hut 11 leave the dining hall and return to their lockdown. He found his man this time. Red satin jacket. Dark, close-cropped hair. His upper lip showed a congenital split under a misshaped nose that looked like a lump of putty. His close-set eyes were fixed on the back of the man before him.

Someone else would see a man. Levon saw a blanket, a coat, and a way out of this place.

22

Gunny Leffertz said:
"Sometimes a show of force is enough."

Levon walked down the broad lane to the latrine and shower building.

A guard stood smoking before the entrance. Levon pointed to his gut and pantomimed gastric distress. The guard snickered. Levon did have an urgent need to go inside; a reaction to the greasy lamb he'd had for breakfast. He needed more time to accustom his digestion to the menu here. The water, too.

New place. New bugs.

The low building was divided between the latrine and the showers. The latrines consisted of a long wooden bench with nine holes cut in the top. The bench was suspended over a concrete trench with a constant stream of water running through it toward an open drain. The system was not ideal, and the building was rank with a fecal and urine stink. The ceiling was open to the joists that supported the roof above. A steel trough sink with three faucets was mounted on the opposite wall. A stack of newspapers sat on the cracked tile floor for those who ran through the single roll of paper given to them each month.

A wall separated the shitter from the shower area. The open entryway was hung with plastic strips. When he was done with what he had gone there to do, Levon parted the strips to inspect the showers.

Unlike the latrine, the shower room had a drop ceiling of painted fiberboard, each panel crusted at the edges with mold. There was a double row of shower stalls in the center of the room, twenty in all. A shower head was suspended above each one from a network of exposed pipes. The stalls were three-sided, with chest-high stainless steel partition walls set to either side in a shared block wall that reached to the ceiling. The place was musky from the smell of stagnant water down in the drains and the sharp pine odor of tar soap. A rolling canvas cart piled high with damp towels rested in a corner.

The door to the latrines squeaked on its hinges. A man grabbed a swatch of newspaper before heading to the nine-holer. Levon exited to the sounds of the man noisily beginning his business.

He'd seen what he needed to see.

Dinner was an oily fish stew served lukewarm with even staler flatbread. The evening call to prayer brayed from the loudspeaker. The occupants of hut 14 were ordered back to their building to be locked in for the night. Levon lagged at the back of the row to watch men who removed their shoes before arranging prayer mats on a concrete pad set for that purpose in front of the dining hall. Bricks arranged in a pattern on the pad's surface formed an arrow pointing to the west/southwest, in the direction of Mecca. A standing basin with running water allowed the men to wash before prayer.

There were fewer than fifty men kneeling to pray. The camp population was primarily Muslim, but most were not observant. The other prisoners respected the praying men by remaining silent and not walking between the supplicants and the city of the Haj. Turkey was still largely secular, although that was changing over time. The era of Ataturk was bowing to the rise of Sharia.

The Prick stood watching the kneeling men, tapping his flail against his leg as though in time to the keening prayer coming from a portable radio. He looked up to see Levon watching him. The men held one another's gaze across the yard until a guard growled at Levon to get inside his hut.

Within the hut, the men had broken into groups to smoke, talk, or play card games. Klaus and Gedde leaned against the wall alongside their cell, sharing something that was making them chuckle. Their smiles faded as Levon approached.

"When do we get a shower?" Levon asked when he reached the cell door.

Klaus did not answer. He looked away, smearing the butt of a cigarette against the bricks of the cell opening. Gedde volunteered to answer.

"It is what, Tuesday? We get a shower on Thursdays. And again on Sunday."

"Is there a rota? More than one hut gets showers each day?" Levon asked.

"Why do you want to know?" Klaus asked.

"Does it hurt to ask?"

"It will hurt someone, I am sure."

Gedde looked from one man to the other, trying to

find the unspoken meaning in their exchange.

"Stinks in here. Just wondering when we get showers." Levon brushed past them to enter the cell.

Inside the cell, the Belgian and his boyfriend sat sharing a cigar, a fat blunt hollowed out and filled with hashish. The Belgian was taking long drags, his belly inflating with the rich smoke, then blowing a stream into the open mouth of the Thai nestled against him. A skunky fog filled the cell. The Corsican lay on his bunk, leafing through a four-year-old *Paris Match* and enjoying the contact high.

Levon stood by the bunk and kicked one of the legs. The Belgian coughed and looked up at him with blood-red eyes.

"Do you know who I am?" The Belgian's voice was hoarse. He spoke French with a Flemish accent.

"The *cochon* who's in my bunk," Levon said.

True to the insult, the Belgian's piggy eyes fixed on Levon.

The Thai giggled. Levon glanced at the other bunk. The boxer was showing a mild interest over the top of his magazine. He pursed his lips and moved a shoulder in a barely perceptible shrug.

Levon's hand moved in a snake-like motion, then he had the Belgian's ear gripped in his fist and pulled the man upright. Bleating, the Thai spilled to the floor. The Belgian followed with a high shriek, rolling atop the smaller man until they were in a scrabbling tangle of limbs.

Levon took a corner of the mattress and blankets and tossed them atop the pair. He unfolded and laid his own blanket on the canvas strapping stretched across the bedframe. Anything was better than sleeping on the floor.

Sputtering, the Belgian clambered to his knees with a stream of curses in Flemish and Dutch. Levon drove the sole of his slipper hard into the fat man's face, and the Belgian dropped back on his ass. A second kick to the face drove his skull against the hard frame of the Corsican's bunk with a meaty crack. His nose was split, and he gargled his own blood. The Thai held a corner of their shared blanket to his face to staunch the flow of the blood and was swatted away.

Levon laid back, his arm behind his head, and studied the crude pornographic drawings carved in the plaster wall by his bunk. He fell asleep listening to the mewling of the Belgian and the whispered comforts offered him by the little Thai.

Hours after lights out, Levon awoke to the weight of someone climbing onto his bed. He turned to see the broad grin of the Thai hovering over him. Levon held a hand up, and the Thai rested his smooth cheek in the open palm with a sigh.

Levering up on one elbow, Levon sent the Thai across the cell as though launched from a catapult. Arms and legs flailing, the smaller man crashed into a wall and came to a landing atop the Belgian, who roared until he was shouted down by voices from the other cells.

Levon rolled himself in his blanket and was quickly asleep once more.

Tomorrow was a hunting day.

23

The cousins found a place to park where they could watch the house and the surrounding acreage. It was a cleared section of ground across the road, and above the horse doctor's property. Weeds had overgrown a section of graded driveway still flat and dry under the cover. There was a concrete pad with piping and PVC electrical conduit jutting up. Someone had planned a house here until their plans were interrupted. A screen of trees hid the van from passersby on the road.

They had sleeping bags, jugs of water, and shopping bags of snack cakes, chips, sodas, and cheese. They had a sack of empanadas as well. Buey had found a place near the interstate. Nowhere near as good as they could get back home, but they were surprised to find them at all in this gringo backwater.

Each took turns watching the house and barn while the other slept or played with their phone. They made a decision to give the watch two days before they moved on the woman. In the end, she would give up the location of the car. The two days was a drop-dead deadline since they owed their pay-up to Uncle

Honesto in three days. They were blood, but that meant nothing if you failed the *plaza* by fucking up or not earning.

And they'd done both.

This bitch would take them to the car and the girl by following her or by force. Time would tell. It damn sure would.

The morning passed slowly. The cousins watched the house through the trees in spells. They played solitaire and killed ninjas and zombies and settled into a Zen-like state of half-wakefulness.

Movement down near the house broke Tesoro from his torpor. He picked up the binoculars to watch the woman walk from the house to her truck, which she climbed into. It started with in fog of blue exhaust. Both men were watching now.

The truck pulled forward and stopped at an angle before going into reverse and disappearing behind the barn. It did not appear on the other side. After a few moments, the truck emerged, pulling a horse trailer. It was white, and decorated with the same logo as appeared on the doors of the truck. The woman pulled to a stop with the rear of the trailer facing the front of the barn. She climbed from the cab and dropped the rear ramp, which also served as a door. She then opened the barn doors and emerged with a buckskin horse with a blond mane. She expertly led the bridled animal up the ramp and into the trailer, where she secured a half-gate in place behind it.

Tesoro admired the woman's handling of the large animal. He had noticed the day before that she was a pretty one, handsome for her age. Her trim body was evident even through her winter clothes. Today her hair was pulled back into a long ponytail that swung back and forth as she worked. Yes, he looked forward to getting to know this woman better.

A second trip into the barn, and she came back out with a dark pony already shaggy with a winter coat. This one gave her more difficulty and needed a slap on the rump to encourage it into the empty stall in the side-by-side trailer. She lifted the ramp back up and shot the bolts to hold it in place, then she secured the barn doors again and pulled forward to the driveway.

"We follow her now, right?" Buey asked.

"To where? She is a doctor. Those are her patients. That is her *ambulancia, ver•a•?*"

"How do you know this?"

"Did you see saddles? She did not take saddles."

Buey's lower lip jutted out, and he tilted his head for a nod.

"I am teaching you something. You see?" Tesoro asked. "We wait until she comes back."

They amused themselves with a farting contest until her return.

* * *

The three hounds loped down the driveway to greet the truck and trail it, baying all the way. The howling turned to tail-wagging when Jessie Hamer pulled up in front of Fern's barn and climbed out.

"That's my mom," Sandy said. "And she's pissed."

They were all three looking out the window at Sandy's mom storming toward the house, boots kicking up gravel. The hounds glided behind her like a wake behind a boat. Uncle Fern met her halfway, with Fella, the ridgeback, by his side. There was a brief exchange, with Jessie pointing to the house. Both disappeared beneath the angle of the porch roof and entered the house.

"Sandy!"

"Oh, crap," Sandy said.

Down in the kitchen, Jessie related for the girls and Fern the visit from the two men the day before, and all the thoughts she'd had throughout a long sleepless night.

"So, anyone have something to tell me?"

A shuffle of feet from the hall foyer and Fella's ears spiking made them all turn to where Esperanza smiled shyly, lost in Merry's oversized sweater.

"Well, if it isn't little Miss Trouble," Jessie said. Her cross expression melted into a warm smile.

* * *

After Merry and Sandy had told Jessie the story of their trip to the mall, the kitchen became a war room. They mapped out a plan of what to do next. Jessie had a general idea of how to proceed, but it was Merry who added her own touch to bring this to a possible conclusion.

Fern made coffee and offered a bowl of last night's half-burned cookies. Jessie noted him reseating himself heavily in his customary captain's chair at the head of the table. He looked tired and a little flushed.

"You feeling okay, Fern?" Jessie said.

"Little touch of reflux, is all," he said, a hand splayed on his chest.

"That coffee won't help that."

"It's fine. I load it up with extra cream."

"Well, *there's* a healthy alternative. Are you having chest pains? Shortness of breath?"

"I thought you were a horse doctor, Jess?"

"Yes, sir. And I went to school longer than your

GP."

"I had a cardiac cath put in two years ago. Healthy as a horse. Just need a few antacids."

"I'd like it better if you went over to the walk-in."

"You girls are going to need me here."

"Not for a while," Jessie countered.

"Thanks, doc, but all I need is a breather," Fern said.

"Stubborn man." Jessie turned to the girls. "I couldn't bring saddles for Montana and Tango. That would have looked like a getaway. But Sandy can ride bareback, and you can saddle Bravo and lead Montana with your new friend on his back."

"You're sure the house is being watched?" Fern asked.

"Ever get that feeling that eyes are on you?" Jessie replied.

"Yeah, I know that feeling all too well. Ignored it one too many times."

"They're watching, trust me. I could feel it in the air like when you know it's gonna rain," Jessie said.

She led the girls out to the trailer. Merry explained it all to Esperanza as they walked. Together, they went into the barn to saddle and bridle Bravo while the Hamers got the mare and pony out of the trailer.

"If you don't know the way, the horses do. What do you think? A two-hour ride along the edge of the watershed?" Jessie asked, handing Montana's reins to Esperanza.

"We'll have cell service part of the way," Sandy said. "We can let you know when we're close."

"It's rough country between here and there. We'll need to take it slow for Esperanza," Merry said.

A scrape of hoofs on gravel, and all turned to watch Esperanza take a fistful of the pony's mane and swing up into an excellent seat on Montana's back. She brushed a strand of hair from her eyes and smiled at their expressions.

"Or not," Jessie said.

* * *

The girls departed, riding up the back trail that led along a gentle slope at the back of the property. The three redbone hounds trotted after, but Uncle Fern whistled and called until the hounds, heads lowered, rejoined him in the yard. The effort taxed him, and he leaned on the fender of Jessie's truck.

"Seriously, old man, you need to be seen," Jessie chided. She pulled open a tool hatch on the side of the truck bed and took out a stethoscope. "Ain't you got enough to think about?" Fern asked. But he parted his shirt front to allow her to listen to his heart.

"Pulse is good if a little fast. Bet your blood pressure is up, too. If it *is* reflux, a nice GI cocktail would make you a whole lot more comfortable."

"Aren't you gonna need me?"

"Only if you're one hundred percent."

"Do I tell them a horse doctor sent me?"

"You *wish* you'd get as good of care as some of the horses I see."

He caved to her and stomped off to his Silverado to head down to Haley and the walk-in clinic there. The hounds followed him down the drive, yelping. They'd turn back when he lost them at the roadway.

"Just you and me now, boy," Jessie said to Fella. He turned his eyes to her, and she swore she could see the primal wisdom there. It was wisdom she prayed, with all her learning and education, she'd not forgotten.

24

Perimeter security was tight. Guards walked the outer fence and manned the towers on a rotating basis. Dogs, big German shepherds, ran the open lane between the fences. What man or animal missed would be caught by the cameras. An escape could get lethal. There was a "shoot to kill" policy in place here. Probably also a graveyard filled with the results of failed attempts.

Within the camp, it was a different story. The guards were laxer about protocol, and even complicit in breaking the rules. More than once, Levon saw guards turn a blind eye to the movement of contraband. Drugs were used openly without punishment. Money passed between prisoners and guards. It was only when the Prick walked the yard that there was any semblance of order. And that was certainly all a sham, the appearance of propriety. The Prick was probably in for the biggest slice of the pie.

Most significant for Levon was that there was never a roll call taken. Except for Hut 11, the prisoners were allowed to roam free within the fence line during daylight hours. They all had to be back "home" and locked in by nightfall, but even then, they were not counted. There was no record of where anyone in the population was at any given time, even after lockdown. As long as they were safely bolted in their huts, the guards were satisfied that all was well.

Showers were scheduled after the morning meal. Three huts showered every three or four days.

Levon walked the lane and sidled over to join the men from Hut 9 as they made their way to the shower side of the building. He entered past a guard whose back was turned. Levon took up a place on the nine-holer. One man was already there, voiding his bowels loudly, and from the wince on his face, painfully. Another joined them, seating himself two holes away, and grunted with satisfaction after a thunderous fart. His cloying aroma joined the rancid stench of the first man.

From the shower section came the hiss of running water and the muffled voices of men. Steam escaped under the doorway. The plastic partition strips ran with condensation.

Feigning interest in a Turkish newspaper, Levon waited out the two men seated either side of him. Once they had left, and before anyone else could enter, Levon stepped atop the long bench. With a standing jump, he was able to get a finger grip on the main roof beam. He levered himself up and walked the joists until he was well over the ceiling of the shower room and out of sight of anyone in the latrine.

The attic area was dark but for shafts of light rising from vents set in the fiberboard ceiling of the room below. Steam rose as well, trapping moist heat in the closed space. Black mold covered the roof beams and made the joists slippery. Levon placed his feet carefully, hands on the angles and uprights for support. The floor of the attic was just the fiberboard set in a metal framework and tacked in place on the crossbeams. One misstep and his foot would crash through.

He found a place and crouched to look down into the shower room through the vanes of a rusted vent. Men were below soaping up or toweling off. The steam was as thick as fog in the morning chill. He crouched lower to see the door to the outside. It was unguarded. The prisoners' clothing hung on steel pegs set in the block wall. Their slippers rested in a neat row atop a shelf just above the floor. A rolling basket of fresh towels had been wheeled into place.

Levon settled himself, feet on a crossbeam and back to an upright. He waited until he heard the hiss dying away below, with a bang of the pipes as the pressure dropped. Crouching again, he watched through the vent as the prisoners of Hut 9, dressed once more, made their way back into the chill air. A few moments passed, and a new gang of men entered—the men of Hut 10. They stripped, showered, dried themselves, and pulled on clothes to depart.

When he was satisfied that the last of the men were gone, Levon made his way to the center of the attic floor. He placed a foot on the fiber board by one of the joists and applied weight to it in a steady pressure. The fiberboard sagged and then parted from the wood, the material soft and cake-like after years of exposure to the damp air. It came away from the heads of the tacks holding it place and swung down like a door, allowing Levon to slip through.

Using the pipes suspended below as a platform to stand on, Levon pressed the fiberboard back in place. It would hold for now. He lowered himself into the shower room. The place was still hazy with steam when the prisoners of Hut 11 entered. Levon was able to hang back in the swirling mist until the men had undressed and begun turning on the showers. The man named Tiryaki was here, entering a shower stall in the row facing away from the rear of the building. He stood in the stream of water and was running the thick block of black soap up his arms less than four paces from where Levon stood in the gloom.

Levon stepped forward and dropped a knotted towel around the smaller man's throat. He turned, pulling hard on the ends of the towel slung over one shoulder. Tiryaki's feet were jerked off the floor as he was levered up on Levon's back. His windpipe pressed closed by the knot crushing his throat, the smaller man kicked out. His feet struck the steel wall of the shower surround in a drumming sound. Levon gave a yank and felt the man's windpipe collapse.

With a heave, Levon bent and turned sharply, the other man's head tight against his shoulder. After a meaty snap, Tiryaki's legs went limp. Levon dropped him to the wet floor with a splash. Men stood in the neighboring stalls with widening eyes and slack mouths.

He was turning to go when a soap-slippery arm snaked around his throat and yanked him across the tiles.

25

"You broke some kind of record, pogue," Gunny
Leffertz said.

Levon turned at the voice coming from the dark, or
as much as he could turn in the box they'd locked him
in. Too short to stand. Too narrow to lie down. Too
cold to sit after the sun went down. All he could do
was crouch, naked and shivering in the frigid thermals
dropping down from the ridgeline of the surrounding
hills.

"Not the first to get out of here, but the farthest.
Long damned run. A lot longer than your first run.
Remember that?"

Levon nodded, remembering.

"Made you a goddamned legend. Got your ass outta
here the first night. Came back the next morning with
huevos rancheros from Mike's for all of us."

Gunny walked around the cage. Levon turned to
keep an eye on him through the chicken wire walls.

"Most pogues follow the path of least resistance.
Follow Seventy-nine north. Head west for the beach,
or south for Mexico. Found one fucker living in a

dumpster behind Mike's place. Living there!"

The man crouched, a hand atop the cage, and leaned close to the wire.

"You went straight up the side of a mountain, over the Coyotes, and crossed a fire road instead of following it. Went around the RV park at Borrego Springs and out into the desert."

Gunny tilted his head as though studying Levon's face.

"Made it all the way to the Salton Sea. Gone two weeks. Two goddamn weeks!"

"My luck ran out, Gunny." Levon spoke low, struggling not to betray that he was shivering.

He'd been living on a boat behind a vacant vacation house in Bombay Beach along the Salton Sea. Survived off the food he found in chest freezers plugged in on back porches, and a vending machine he managed to pry open at the Ski Inn. He set some dogs to barking, and a neighbor called the highway patrol. They knew right away from his bleached white BDUs that he had come out of the training site at Warner Springs. Gunny Leffertz was there when they took him out of the prowl car, wrists and ankles flex-cuffed.

"Welcome back to SERE, hillbilly."

Now he was on his second day and third night in the cage. Broil by day and freeze by night with a bottle of water and a HooAH! bar twice a day.

"You gonna try to leave here again, pogue?" Gunny Leffertz asked. He plucked the wire with a callused finger, making it twang.

"That's my job, Gunny."

"You hate me, don't you, pogue?"

"You're just doing your job, Gunny."

"Out there. Downrange. In the wicked world,

there's men might do worse to you. Worse'n me. You gonna hate them? They just doing their job?"

Levon remained silent, eyes on his own reflection in the Gunny's dark lenses.

"You need to hate them. Have to hate them. Can't kill a man you don't hate. Can't kill a fucker you don't look down on. Kinda asshole that can kill without hate is worse'n an animal. But you have to hate smart. You know what I'm talking about?"

"Get angry. Get stupid. Get killed, Gunny."

Gunny let out a dry chuckle.

"You and me are gonna have breakfast together. Gonna talk about your future over biscuits and gravy."

In spite of himself, Levon's mouth watered.

"See you at sunrise, pogue," Gunny said and rose to walk away into the greater dark.

26

"I need to piss," Buey said.

Tesoro nodded. He sat behind the wheel, eyes on the road and the driveway that led to the horse lady's house.

Buey stepped from the van to stretch before heading into the woods to pee. A movement in the corner of his eye made him turn. He tried to pull the handgun he kept tucked in the waistband of his jeans, but it snagged on the lining of his coat. The motion plucked the Glock from his fingers to spin away. He dropped to hands and knees to find it in dried leaves that carpeted the ground.

The pressure on his bladder was urgent, but his need to find that gun was even more pressing. There were sounds of footfalls, something moving with great care through the woods above him. His hand found the pistol. He brought it up in the direction of the movement.

A deer, a big eight-pointer, stood munching and eyeing Buey over the trembling front sights. His ears twitched forward. Body tensed to run. In the trees behind the buck, Buey could see more deer moving, does and fawns. The honking of the van's horn scattered them. They vanished into the birches as if they were never there.

"I still have to piss!" Buey shouted. He struggled to pull down his zipper, the Glock still in his fist. The horn honked again and he started, sending a yellow stream down one leg of his jeans. It splashed on the hand holding the pistol. Buey hissed and cursed and urged the urine from his body. The horn bleated behind him a third time. Jamming the damp pistol back in place, he hobbled back to the van and a cursing Tesoro.

"The car! The Kia! It's here!" Tesoro said and threw the van into gear. Buey was only halfway in when it took off, back wheels spraying dirt.

***

Jessie brought the minivan to a slewing stop in front of the barn.

She was out of it and racing. Somewhere a horn was honking. She threw the barn doors wide and ran to where Scarlett, a roan quarter horse mare stood in the corridor between the stables, cross-reined and ready to ride.

Jessie undid the snaps keeping the animal in place and swung up on her back with a whispered apology for leaving her saddled so long. A little kick and a snap of the reins, and the mare bolted forward. Jessie ducked to clear the door and pressed with her left knee to turn the horse right.

She twisted in the saddle to look back. That shitbox van was roaring up her driveway. Rooster-tails of dust rose behind it. Jessie bent low, her face pressed to the neck of the mare, her ears filled with her breathing.

Scarlett was cantering for the trail that started at the opening in the back fence. She knew the path well since she'd been ridden along it a dozen times in the past month. She was boarding at Riverstone while her owners were away in Europe. Beyond her pasture time, either Jessie or Sandy got her out for exercise three or four times a week. To her, this was fun.

Jessie gave the horse her head, and they raced from the paddock across the open pasture that skirted the wooded slope. It was only ten acres, and they would cross it in seconds. It still felt like a mile run, the shelter of the trees an impossible distance away.

The van kept on, coming off the driveway with a bounce. The opening in the paddock fence was not quite wide enough. There was a shriek of metal as it squeezed between the stout upright posts, the ends of the cross rails leaving long gouges the length of the van.

Slewing and swaying, the van came on across the pasture, rebuilding speed after the hitch at the fence opening. It was closing on the woman and the horse racing for the tree line. The horse was at a full gallop now. Clods of turf flew in the air behind her hooves. The van was close enough that one of the divots exploded across its windshield.

And then they were into the trees, Scarlett powering up the slope to leave the van behind.

* * *

Tesoro jerked to a stop and leapt from the van at the foot of the wooded hillside. He kicked at the dirt, then tore off his coat and threw it to the ground.

Buey watched his cousin shake a fist and shout a

stream of abuse and dire threats at the surrounding forest. Tesoro turned back to see a ragged furrow along the van's side. A long strip of chrome trim swayed like a feeler. Buey was drying his Glock with his shirttail when Tesoro returned to the van to bang on the door.

"We go back to the house!"

"What for?"

"To rob it! To burn it down! I do not know!"

Tesoro circled the van back and paused while Buey walked backward through the fence opening, guiding him through the narrow gap. They parked between the barn and house, leaving the engine running.

"I will look in the house. You search the car," Tesoro said. He was on his way to the ranch house at a trot.

"What do I look for?" Buey called to him.

"Clues! Evidence! Something to tell us where we might find the girl!"

We are detectives now, Buey thought as he neared the Kia. *I am Columbo or from CSI looking for fibers or a receipt*. He wanted to ask more questions, but his cousin was not in the mood. He pulled the driver-side door open and was startled by a piercing squeal that turned into an insistent warble. It was painful, so he clapped hands over his ears and backed away from the minivan. The annoying sound continued. The car's lights were flashing.

He turned back to the house. Tesoro was running from the porch, stabbing a finger at their van and shouting. Buey removed a hand from one ear to hear what he was saying. Over his cousin's unintelligible ranting, he could hear a new sound—the rising and falling wail of a siren coming from the house. Along with it was a basso Anglo male voice coming from loudspeakers. He could not understand the voice, but recognized the tone as "get the fuck out!"

The cousins clambered into their ride and took off, leaving the cacophony from the house and car to echo up the holler.

* * *

Jessie Hamer sat astride Scarlett and smiled as she tapped her cell phone. From the floor of the valley came the woop-woop, squee-squee of her house and car alarms, as well as the Sam Elliott voice informing any intruders that the police had been called, although they hadn't. She'd stopped paying for the monthly service years before. She relied instead on the alarm to provide a wake-up and ten-second head start to retrieve the .38 she kept in a gun safe by her bed—the Smith & Wesson that now rested comfortably in the clamshell holster, snug in the small of her back.

She pulled the reins and turned her mount to face the source of a huff and a grunt from the trail above. The soft thump of hooves reached her through the birches long before she could see the girls walking the horses in a row toward her. They were beaming as they joined her, their little adventure ending in victory.

But that wasn't the end of the adventure. They'd skunked the two *hombres* looking for Merry and Sandy's little *amiga*. That didn't mean they'd lost them forever.

So now what?

27

The chokehold was strong but inexpert.

Levon tucked his chin into the crook of a meaty arm furred with ginger hair, which kept the grip off his throat. It was the heavyset Euro with the red beard he'd seen earlier. The pressure on Levon's jaw grew as the bigger man put his back into it.

Levon pushed hard off a shower upright with both feet. This caused the man gripping him from behind to lose his footing on the soap-slick floor and they both crashed to the tiles, with Redbeard taking the brunt of it. Levon twisted to slam an elbow into the bigger man's ribs. Three lightning jabs, and Redbeard released him with a grunt. Levon rolled off, only to spring back, driving the heel of one hand up under the man's jaw. Redbeard's shaven skull struck the tiles with a crack.

Avoiding his grasping hands, Levon got a double grip on the man's right wrist. He drove his slippered foot into the man's throat, pressing down as he hyper-extended the captured arm. The bigger man flopped and twisted but couldn't shake Levon off. A pinching grip on the ball of the man's hand dislocated his thumb. Redbeard howled through clenched teeth, spittle spraying from his lips to fleck his beard with foam. His face turned crimson, then purple as Levon's weight cut off his air supply. His tongue was blue and lashing out between gnashing teeth filmed with blood.

The guy fought like a gaffed marlin until, starved for oxygen, his eyes turned red, the blood vessels bursting.

Levon kept the pressure in place, sweeping his eyes around the half-circle of men standing in the warm mist and watching the action.

One, an evil-looking man with stripes of raised scar tissue across his torso and arms, began to step forward from the group. A knife fighter. Levon caught the gleam of a needle-shaped blade in his fist, a homemade weapon of hammered spring steel with a duct-tape grip.

Levon released Redbeard, unconscious, comatose, or worse, to lie lifeless in a spreading puddle of his own piss. He crouched to receive the first attack from the knife man. An older man, with a snow white mustache, took hold of the man's knife arm.

"Chay-chon," the older guy said.

The Chechen.

The knife man stopped, eyeing Levon. Nodding once, he flicked his hand in a practiced move, and the blade vanished. The group broke up, returning to their showers.

Levon walked to the partition door and shoved through the plastic strips. He was soaked to the skin, and his shirt was stuck to him under his coat. He exited into the morning light through the latrine exit. It was colder outside, and he held the coat closed tight around him. The guard outside turned to him with a question.

"*Diyare. Boklar,*" Levon said with a grunt. The shits.

The guard snorted and returned his attention to his cigarette.

Levon went back to his cell and stripped off his wet clothing to rub himself down with his blanket. Wrapped in the blanket, he squatted over a drain in the floor to wring out his shirt and pants.

"Murder looks like hard work," Klaus said from where he leaned, arms folded, in the cell doorway.

"They find the bodies?" Levon twisted the clothing in his hands. Water bled into the drain.

"You went on a spree?"

"It got complicated."

"There has been no alarm raised."

"There will be."

"All this for a coat and blanket?" Klaus asked.

"*Woher hast ɪu ɪeinen mantel unɪ ɪeine ɪecke?*" Levon asked.

"*Meine mutter.*"

"My mommy's not here. I'm on my own."

There were shouts outside, but the growing clamor was cut short by orders shouted over the camp's loudspeakers. Clubs hammered on the walls of the hut.

"*Hücrelerinize ɪönün!*" Return to your cells.

The rest of the men of Hut 14 shuffled inside, hurried along by curses and threats. The door was bolted and locked behind them. The men of Levon's cell stepped into the cramped quarters, ignoring him as he hung his damp clothes from a wire stretched between the bunks.

There was no afternoon meal that day. Klaus eyed Levon sullenly but said nothing.

28

"Why do you think you're here, pogue?" Gunny Leffertz asked.

"At SERE, Gunny?" Levon was wolfing down scrambled eggs, bacon, and biscuits and gravy. Gunny topped off Levon's tumbler of fresh-squeezed orange juice before pouring himself a mug of coffee.

"At SERE, sure. And Colombia. And sniper school at Pendleton. *All* your advanced weapons training. Why you?"

"Uncle Sam always needs us big, dumb country boys, Gunny."

"That is right. You are right. The services always call on you rednecks, hicks, and hoopies. Between you and the Indians, that's the backbone of this country's fighting force. You know, if the general population signed on the dotted line at the rate the tribes do, we'd have never needed a draft? You serve with a few redskins, pogue?"

"A few. A Pima helped me through jump school at Benning. You a country boy yourself, Gunny?"

"Mississippi born and bred, pogue. The Marines get

plenty of your kind. But not your quality."

"I think maybe this is where God wants me to be, Gunny."

"He sure built you for the mission. You sailed through boot like a trip to the state fair. Your intelligence tests, physical acuity, memory, and language abilities are among the highest on record. Tests prove you have an eidetic memory. You'd have crushed West Point and Annapolis if you'd been born anywhere else but Bumfuck, Alabama."

"I hated school, Gunny."

"Well, your ass is in the classroom now. You ever wonder what the end of the road looks like for you? What's the end result here?"

"God and the Marines have a plan for me, I guess, Gunny."

"You know what a hunter/killer is, pogue?"

"I know a little. Special unit that hunts and kills terrorists. Delta. Phoenix. That kind of deal, Gunny?"

"Right. But the program I'm part of has no name. We go by a prefix to a number assigned to each op."

"What's the mission, Gunny?"

"We kill…*you* kill…this country's enemies."

"That's what I signed up for. When do I start, Gunny?"

"You've still got a ways to go, and things to learn. Finish your breakfast, and get a shower and some rack time. We'll talk more later." Gunny stood to leave.

"Thank you, Gunny."

"You're welcome, son. You're welcome."

29

Tesoro and Buey wound up in trouble with the cops anyway.

Deputy Brandon "Brando" Sawtell sat in his county car and read off the license plate of the piece-of-shit Econoline he had pulled over onto the grassy verge of Hood Road.

"Maryland. Tee-one-one. Bee-five-seven. Commercial van."

As he called in to dispatch, he was keeping an eye on the van. It was all banged up down either side, and the right rear light housing had been torn free. That was the proximate cause for his call-over. He was also entering the same info into the laptop mounted on the dash next to his shotgun. He was searching the JMD database for state or federal warrants.

"Unit Bravo two-two?"

Sounded like Bernice Tolliver on the horn this afternoon. She was a no-bullshit multiple grandma on her third husband. The 'bama drawl and two packs of Merits a day gave her voice a comforting authority.

"Go ahead for two-two."

"That vehicle is registered to an Armand Peter Engstrom of Annapolis. There are no current warrants. Do you need further assistance?"

"Wouldn't hurt. This ride looks like it's been through the wars."

"Roger that."

"Going to talk to the driver."

"Be careful, honey."

Brando watched the driver-side mirror as he approached the van. Light traffic on the two-lane for this time of day on a Saturday. Passing cars and pickups gave the county car and its quarry a wide berth. He could see the guy behind the wheel in the mirror, smiling as their eyes met. Smilers were trouble. Nodders were worse.

He had been home nearly ten years after getting out of the Army, but all the wiring was still there. He got the same tingle up his spine off this stop as he had gotten approaching intersections or crossing bridges back in Iraq. That hard-learned situational awareness was sending all the signals, the board in his mind lit up red straight across.

He moved to an angle to the driver side bumper. It gave him a view of the van's dark interior, as well as the driver and passenger. Mexicans, by his eye. And not pickers. Wrong time of year for it. And the shaved back-and-sides fauxhawks gave them away as players.

"License and registration."

"Yes, sir. Right here, sir." The beefy one behind the wheel offered the papers. Brando lowered his Ray-Bans to inspect them.

"Which one of you is Armand Engstrom?"

"I am," the driver said. His smile stretched wider but never reached his eyes. The younger guy in the suicide seat watched with sleepy eyes and lips parted. A dummy playing dumber.

"Were you aware that you're missing a rear taillight? And I see now that your windshield is cracked."

"We were just on our way to have it repaired, sir."

"Did you have an accident, Mr. Engstrom?"

The driver looked at the passenger, who gave a shrug, eyes alert now and squinting.

"My cousin left it in gear and it rolled into a…a… what do you call it?"

"I wouldn't know, Mr. Engstrom. What *o* you call it?"

"*Una zanja*," the passenger offered.

"*¡Sí!* Yes! A ditch. The van rolled into a ditch!"

"There were no other vehicles involved? Any property damage?"

Both men shook their heads.

"Are either or both of you foreign nationals?" Brando asked, remaining where he was by the bumper.

"You are not allowed to ask us that," the driver said. His surprise was turning to offense.

"I can ask you anything I like, Mr. Engstrom, and I suggest you answer truthfully."

"But in Maryland…"

"You and your cousin aren't in Maryland, Mr. Engstrom. This is Alabama, and I am within my rights to ask you about your citizenship. Are either or both of you foreign nationals?"

The men in the van offered assurances that they were natives of the Eastern Shore. They were both nodding like bobbleheads. Brando's hand found its way to the butt of his service piece all on its own.

"I'm gonna have to ask both of you gentlemen to place your hands on the dashboard," Brando said. His thumb undid the snap securing his Colt in place.

The driver's smile stretched wider, showing his molars. Sweat beaded on his face. The passenger's mopey expression deepened to a scowl, and his hand moved out of sight.

"Hands on the dash," Brando directed, each word a sentence on its own. The 1911 in his gloved fist and trained at the van's occupants through the windshield provided the final punctuation.

A Haley Police Department Tahoe glided to a place behind Brando's cruiser, lights going.

Two hours later, Mr. Engstrom and his cousin were booked for criminal possession of unregistered firearms, driving with a fraudulent license, and receiving stolen goods. Once they were printed and their pictures had been taken, a whole plethora of federal warrants sprang from the Pandora's box of the DOJ's criminal reference system. ICE was called, and Herman Guillermo Ruiz and Jose Angel "Buey" Ruiz were packed off to the field office in Hoover to face further charges, imprisonment, and deportation.

30

As preposterous as it sounded, the official story was that the two men in the showers killed one another in a fight.

The witnesses on the scene supported that version. A lover's spat turned deadly. The camp administrators did not have sufficient interest or curiosity to look into the matter further. The dead prisoners were degenerate criminals who took one another's lives. End of story. End of report.

Still, some show of authority was called for to address this break in order. The prisoners were rousted from their huts before the evening meal. They stood in rows along either side of the main lane. The camp's commander, with The Prick by his side, spoke to them through a bullhorn. The commander, an officious little man in a sharply creased military uniform, was rarely seen outside the admin building. He was pale, and had a pencil-thin mustache and rimless glasses like a Nazi from a movie. A too-large cap encrusted with gold braid completed the image. His voice matched his image: reedy and halting.

He explained to the population that every death is regrettable, even that of the least among us. And he wasn't about to tolerate any breakdown in the routine established here. The guard would be doubled for the foreseeable future, and a guard would be posted inside the showers as well as outside from now on. If they insisted on acting like animals, they would be treated as animals. Infractions would be dealt with swiftly and harshly, blah, blah, and on and on and on until the little man ran out of threats and bullshit. He handed the bullhorn off to the Prick, who called out the numbers of the first huts to go to supper.

Levon met Ball Boy coming out of the dining hall as he was going in.

"We talk soon, yes?" Ball Boy said in his gutter French.

Levon nodded and brushed past for that evening's offering of lamb and some kind of greens.

* * *

Snow flurries were drifting over the football pitch the next day. It didn't slow the play; both sides charged up and down the lumpy field in pursuit of the yellow and blue ball.

"I need that phone," Levon said. He stood with Ball Boy at the corner of the field farthest from the quartet of guards huddled to watch the play.

"You need earn phone," Ball Boy said. A yellow cigarette waggled in his lips as he spoke.

"I did what you asked."

"That was for blanket. Coat. You are paid."

"It's not enough."

"I speak to *chef*. I ask maybe something else for you? Cigarette? The drugs? To fuck? Have boy pretty like woman. Same thing."

"All I want is a phone."

"Is expensive, phone. You need earn phone."

"Tell me how and I'll earn it."

Ball Boy blew a stream of smoke at the ground, then turned his head to look at the Chechen sitting bundled up on his lawn chair. The muscle poured a mug of sweet coffee for the boss man. The big man had a swatch of white bandage taped across his face, over a steel splint to hold his nose in place.

"I bring you something you like. Later."

Levon nodded before walking away.

Later that day, he found a Danish porn magazine on his bunk. A blonde with an idiot leer pressed her breasts together on the cover. When he picked it up to toss it to the floor, a folded slip of paper fell out. He retrieved it and opened it.

Mehmet Sarıkoğlu

2

31

Honesto Camarillo was tired of the business of drugs and whores.

This had nothing to do with pangs of conscience. It was just that *narcos* and *putas* brought risks with them. Risks from the law, and from the competition. And, by their very nature, these two illicit ventures could make a man crazy. It was tempting to wallow in the world of sin that surrounded both.

He longed to build something lasting. Something clean. Something legitimate. For him, this took the form of multiple businesses under the umbrella of Dixie-Pro Industries Ltd. Dixie-Pro was incorporated in Wyoming, with its world headquarters in Birmingham, Alabama. He had a logo, business cards, and an ad in the Yellow Pages. You couldn't have *those* with drugs and whores.

From the window of his world headquarters—a trailer equipped with a desk, a sofa, filing cabinets, a mini-fridge, and an assignment board—Honesto could survey his empire. It was comprised of four unmarked vans, a panel truck, and two tow trucks parked in front of a garage building. It was all enclosed in a chain link fence, with vinyl slats interwoven to hide it from the view of the street and the VFW hall next door.

Dixie-Pro was, according to Google Maps, a thriving business offering roadside repair, towing, plumbing, electrical work, and roofing. D-P had twenty-two locations in the Birmingham suburbs and surrounding counties. Virtually, that is. Honesto registered these locations with Google, whose verification process was iffy at best. In truth, the trailer, garage, and small fleet of vehicles were the only assets the company had, and the lot behind the VFW was their only location. The other offices were either phony addresses, or the addresses of legitimate businesses like nail salons and pizzerias that had agreed to allow their locales to be used in exchange for a few bucks or some favors.

Calls and texts to those disparate locations were all routed to the row of cellphones he kept on his desk. If you were stranded in the breakdown lane on 65 near Homewood and it was raining cats and dogs, your phone would assure you that there was a Dixie-Pro Towing service just five minutes away. Your commode backs up and company's coming for dinner at your house in Sandusky? Well, Dixie-Pro Plumbing's just a hop, skip, and a jump from your house. In reality, help might be an hour or more away, but most callers sat tight with their first choice. It's Google Maps. It has to be right, right?

And, of course, the "pro" in Dixie-Pro was a bit of an exaggeration. Honesto's employees were Juans of all trades but *jefes* of none. One call, they were an electrician, and the next, a car mechanic. The only consistency was the payment method: cash only. Dixie-Pro wanted no part of credit card companies or banks. You pay *inero* or nothing. Yankee Dollar, Homer. Pay up, or sit in the rain on the roadside. Pony up, or live with a lake of shit in your *baño*. Don't like the service? Yelp all you want. Dixie-Pro was virtually, if not literally, all over the map, and there was always another sucker.

This was better than whores and dope, and it was legal, if not strictly ethical. And it had the advantage of being high tech, something with a future. Honesto already had plans to expand into Tennessee and Georgia. A hundred Dixie-Pros. A thousand. There was no end to it, like Starbucks or McDonalds.

But for now, it was still a dream in its infancy. For now, he still had to deal with the less tasteful trades. And also, he had this headache from his *pen*ejo* nephews. Picked up by the police. Their asses shipped back to Chinobampo. To top it off, they lost the girl they were running. Honesto had paid good money for that *niña*, money she had only begun to earn back for him.

Sure, it was a loss he could absorb over time, but there was a principle here. He could not have a *chica* he had paid for go running into the hills. The others would hear somehow and go running too. And, until Dixie-Pro was up and running with more locations, he was still in the whore business. He could not afford a diaspora of *putas* taking off for home, or perhaps other markets.

But he lacked the manpower to hunt the little one down. His men were all busy tending to their own jobs for the *plaza*. Running girls, running dope. Those that weren't pimping and pushing were pretending to be plumbers and garage door repairmen.

He sipped coffee and smoked and thought about

this problem between calls for service. He stood at the window and watched a couple of his men climb into vans and another into a tow truck and pull out of the lot. Rolling cash machines was what they were. He would have a fleet one day. His thoughts moved to daydreaming about the time when he would have a secretary to take the calls. She would have long blonde hair down to her ass and tits out to here, and sometimes, when it was not so busy—

The door banged open and one of the drivers came in. A Honduran named Matías, or maybe Martín. Mateo?

"What is it? Your van is okay?" Honesto growled. Repairs for his piece-of-shit vehicles were his biggest headache in this venture.

"No, *jefe*. The van is fine. *Primo*. I only ask for a favor," Matías, Martín, or Mateo said. He clutched a piece of white paper in his hand.

Honesto twirled a hand in impatience. He wanted to get back to the secretary who, in his mind, had just dropped to her knees behind his desk.

"My son. His dog has run away. I only ask if I can put a notice up on your board. Maybe one of the drivers see the dog?"

"Yes, yes. Go ahead."

"*Muchas gracias, jefe! Muchas gracias!*" The man borrowed a pin from the tray under the assignment board and put up the notice, a photo of a little beagle held in the arms of a junior image of Matías, Martín, or Mateo wearing an idiot grin.

"*De na•a!* Now get out!" The Honduran did so, the door banging shut in his wake.

His mood was ruined. The vision of himself and the blonde—he'd named her Cathy—was not coming back into the clear focus he'd achieved before. He stepped to the board to examine the new notice.

The dog's name was Bucky. There was a description in bad Spanish and worse English. Along the bottom, the paper was sliced into fringes. On each was a handwritten phone number. Honesto's fingers played with the fringes, ruffling them.

A smile creased his face.

32

Amalia Maria Guzman had walked a mile from the factory gate, with two more miles to go until she was home. She wondered how much longer she could do this.

It did not matter. It had to be done, and there was no one else but her to do it. Ten hours or more of sewing sneaker tops on the machines at the *maquila▪ora* and three hours walking each day. She left in the dark, and returned home in the dark. She walked with a group of other women from the Koo-Ding plant, their number becoming smaller and smaller as they turned into side streets where their homes were located. Closer to the plant, they met women walking the opposite way on the other side of the street. On their way to the overnight shift. All wore the sky-blue work smocks provided by the plant.

Amalia envied those women, who got to work in the cool of the evening, the dark hours passing by unseen outside the windowless factory floor. The nights were so long at home. She had a list of chores before she could sleep. Her mother made meals and kept the kitchen, and that was a godsend, but the children always needed something done. Help with schoolwork. A story to be read. And Carlos often needed her for one thing or another. He was growing weaker over time. The doctors said it was cancer, but Carlos would not tell her what kind. It was better for her not to worry, and after all, what did it matter? They had no money for treatment.

Finally, the last of the women walking her way had left the main road, and Amalia walked alone. The narrow lanes filled with noisy motorbikes and tuk-tuk taxis gave way to an eastbound roadway lined on either side with single-story buildings with metal roofs. Here only the occasional farm truck passed. The scenery was drab. The colorful signs and storefronts of Jalapa were replaced by unfinished structures of concrete block. It was in one of these sprawling apartments that she lived with her husband and children.

A Jeep with its top down caught her in its headlights and slowed to travel alongside her. She hurried her walk. Young men, bare arms black with tattoos, whistled and called to her, but she would not turn her face to them. They apparently decided she was too old and too used for further attention. Engine whining, they tore away, leaving her choking in a plume of dust. She walked on along the edge of the dark roadway, alone with her thoughts once more.

She imagined the day Carlos would be taken from her and felt relief. She would pray then for forgiveness. Such a terrible thing to think. Such a selfish thing to wish for. But her mind would wander from the prayers to thoughts of how she could move back to where her mother and sisters lived up in the mountains. The children would be away from the city, with its noise and temptations and dangers. They could live a cleaner life in the mountains.

It was a fantasy. One brand of poverty traded for another.

The hard-baked lane that led to her home came up on her right. She turned off to walk under the *ciebas*, their branches creaking in the night wind that stirred at the foot of the surrounding mountains. The sad rows of apartments sat beyond, their exteriors once bright pinks and blues, now faded and peeling, crisscrossed with spray-painted names.

A car sat athwart the road. It was a *Norte Americano* car, broad and long and shiny with chrome. The engine purred. Muted sounds came from within. A radio was playing. She turned her eyes away as she made to walk past it. She heard the clunk of a lock, and the door opening to let the sound from within out. A football game, a shrieking announcer, *vuvuzelas* honking and the surf-like roar of a crowd. A light from inside the car threw her shadow long across the sandy lot, pointing like a compass needle at the two-room *apartamento pequeño* where her family lived.

A shadow joined hers, then another. She closed her eyes to pray once more.

* * *

They spoke outside under the pole lamp, moths making dancing shadows that dappled the ground.

Two young men were in tight white tank tops and baggy army pants. Their bodies were covered in black ink, even up their throats and on their shaved scalps. A third man remained in the back seat of the car. Amalia could not see his face in the shadows, only the glow of his cigar.

"Your daughter has run away," one of the young men said. A gold cross with a brass bullet attached to it dangled on a chain around his neck. He had a lit hand-rolled cigarette in his mouth. The smoke smelled sickly-sweet.

Amalia could not understand at first. She looked, blinking, from one to the other.

"She has run away from her *jefe*. She is hiding from him."

"Where? Where is this?"

"In Alabama."

The word meant nothing to Amalia. Was this a place?

"*Los Esta•os Uni•os.* It is a place in the USA." It was the other young man, a skeletal figure with sad eyes.

"We gave you money for her." This from the boy wearing the bullet cross.

Panic rose in Amalia. The mention of money, the price paid for her daughter, made her touch her own cross. Her fingers went to the tiny pewter crucifix she wore pinned to her smock.

"The money is gone. My husband is sick. Very sick. And I have other children."

"You have a son close to Esperanza's age," Bullet Cross said.

Her daughter's name coming from this boy's mouth was like a dagger in her chest. For a moment, she did not understand the mention of her son, what it meant. The boy with the profaned cross was still speaking. Amalia struggled to follow his words.

"We will be repaid. One way or the other, you owe us for this. It is on you. The boy is not worth as much as a girl, but he is something."

Amalia stepped toward the men. Her knees were

weak. Her mind was racing.

"You understand?" Sad Eyes this time. "If you cannot give us back your daughter, then we must take your son."

"How am I to do this? Esperanza is in All-Obama. I have no way to find her. She cannot come home."

"She will call you. You will tell us where to find her."

"Call me? Call here? How? We have no phone." Amalia waved a hand at the dark buildings behind her. A dog was barking inside one of the apartments.

"Here. She will call you on this." Sad Eyes stepped closer to place a silver lozenge in her hand. He used both his hands to press her fingers around it.

"I have no money for this. I have no way to keep it charged. There's no electric here."

"It's all paid for. You don't worry about that. Just keep the phone switched on and charged." Bullet Cross was becoming impatient with her. He tapped his sneakered foot.

"Use this. Connect it where you work." Sad Eyes handed her a loop of black cord with a boxy plug on one end.

"I am not sure I can do this. I don't think it's allowed," Amalia protested. She flipped up the top of the phone, and it beeped. On a tiny screen was a picture of a sunny day on a sandy beach lined with palm trees and pearly surf.

"Goddamn, *puta!*" Bullet Cross dashed his joint to the ground and whirled away in frustration.

"Find a way. Keep the phone charged and with you at all times," Sad Eyes said. "Your *niña* will call. We will be back, and you tell us where to find her."

"*Vamanos,*" Bullet Cross said and stormed back to the jeep.

"Do not lose the phone," Sad Eyes ordered in farewell.

Amalia nodded mutely, clutching the phone and charger to her breast with one hand. The fingers of the other rubbed the crucifix in unconscious prayer. The bright lights swept over her, the tires sending up a fresh cloud of dust. She stood and watched the red lights vanish into the screen of trees. She was still there mouthing silent prayers as she heard the car's engine build to a whine out on the valley road.

* * *

The next day in the blink-and-you-miss-it town of Colby, Alabama, Dale Little stood looking at a photocopied notice stapled to the utility pole outside Fay's diner.

Dale had had little to do since they shut down the Kubota dealership over in Teeter. He'd been a mechanic there, fixing the lawn mowers and chainsaws and trimmers that came in, but business had slowed down a year back, and the place was shuttered. Dale figured it might reopen, with all the new gated developments getting started along the county road down to Haley. Until then, he'd bide his time and watch Netflix back at his mom's house. But some days, he'd had enough of her bitching and whining and walked down into town for a Coke and a quiet smoke, or to catch up with some of the other out-of-work guys hanging at the E & B barber shop.

Any distraction was welcome.

The flyer showed a photograph of a pretty little girl smiling in a white dress. She held flowers in her hands. Looked Mexican to Dale's eyes. In English and Spanish, the flyer asked if anyone had seen the girl, and requested that any information on her whereabouts be reported to the number below. The bottom of the flyer was cut into a row of tabs, each bearing a phone number.

Dale tore one off and held it close to his eyes to inspect it. He'd left his Walgreen's reading glasses back at the house when his mother's carping drove him out.

The row of digits on the strip of paper was one long-ass telephone number. He folded the strip of paper into the watch pocket of his jeans and vowed to keep a sharp eye out for the little *bonita*. This solemn vow faded away when Dale joined a spirited discussion at the barber shop about the Tide's chances at the Orange Bowl.

33

Gunny Leffertz said:
"There ain't a man on this Earth can't be got."

"I will not help you! *Lass mich alleine!*" Klaus said. He was storming away from Levon across the gravel yard.

"All I'm asking is who's in Hut Two?" Levon said. His long strides brought them even.

Klaus came to halt only because to proceed farther would have taken him in front of the rows of men kneeling at final prayer. He turned back to slide between two huts. Levon followed.

"You want me to help you spill more blood?" he asked, hands shaking as he fumbled a cigarette from a box drawn from an inside pocket.

"What should you care?" Levon asked. He struck a stick match and held it for the German. He had to take Klaus' hand in his to steady it for the touch of the flame.

"I do not! They were scum! This is different!" Klaus took a long drag.

"How? How is it different?"

"Hut Two is dissidents, men opposed to the current

regime. Erdoğan has them locked up here to silence them."

"Who are they?"

"Politicians. Journalists. Anyone who speaks against the president."

"I never see them. They're protected, like the deviants and the rats?"

"They are vulnerable to attack, same as Hut Fourteen. They are kept apart because a murder of a known figure would be an embarrassment. Ankara wants these men forgotten about. Their deaths would not go unnoticed."

"He'll be harder to get at than Tiryaki."

"Who is the man?"

"Mehmet Sadıkoğlu."

"Very hard. This man writes for a magazine that is popular. He is often on television. He is protected. His death would be a blot on the president. The world would take notice."

"Why would the Chechen want a man like that dead? He doesn't seem political."

"He's not. But there's hardliners who want Sadıkoğlu dead. They would pay a fortune to have him eliminated."

Levon stood looking down at flecks of snow swirling over the gravel.

"You will kill him for a phone." Klaus hawked and spat.

"They won't allow me to contact my consulate. I need that contact."

"Enough for a man to die?"

"I'm not going to kill him."

"You're *not* going to kill anyone?"

"I didn't say that."

Klaus blinked snowflakes from his eyes to stare at Levon.

34

"This man will take over where I left off, Slick," Gunny Leffertz said.

They were on a naval base at Dam Neck, Virginia. Summer sunlight streamed in through the blinds of the common room. The three men sat at a table with mugs of fresh-brewed coffee, and all wore in civvies. Levon had on an Ocean City, Delaware lifeguard squad t-shirt and board shorts. Gunny was in khakis and the world's ugliest guayabera shirt. The third man wore a black polo shirt and cargo pants. He was an Asian man whom Gunny introduced as Brett Tsukuda.

"The SEALs tell me you're half-fish," Tsukuda said. He had an easy smile. He removed tinted shades to meet Levon's gaze.

"Gunny said he'd probably try and drown me, sir."

"No need for the 'sir,' Levon. Call me Brett. I don't hold rank." Brett poured a stream of sugar into his mug.

"You gonna eat that or drink it?" Levon asked.

"I like it sweet," Brett said, stirring the syrup with a spoon.

"You're with an agency."

"Doesn't matter which one, does it? It's all just alphabet soup. We trade personnel like farm team baseball."

"Brett runs the shit list," Gunny said. "He points and you shoot. You're gonna see places you never heard of."

"Al Qaeda and its affiliate groups are global. They're set up everywhere but Antarctica," Brett explained.

"Gunny says this unit has a code suffix but no name. Will I be part of a team?"

"You are the unit, Levon. You are the team. You'll work with different hunter/killer outfits, but they'll only be support for you. You're the headliner, and they're your backup band."

"They won't even know your name, Slick. We have a dozen IDs for you to use. Your show. You take down the target, you adios like a shadow."

"Will any of the targets be domestic?" Levon asked. His eyes were locked on Tsukuda's.

"Yes."

"Any American citizens?"

"That a problem for you?" Brett asked, unblinking.

"Not for me."

"You'll be covered, son," Gunny said. He leaned across the table and gripped Levon's arm. "No one will know your name but us three at this table. There won't be any consequences for these kills."

"They're all bad actors. All righteous marks. Every one of them is a clear and present danger," Brett said.

"Just asking. I need to know the rules. Even the ones I'll be breaking."

Brett looked at Gunny Leffertz to gauge his reaction. The man kept his gaze locked on Levon with an intensity that made Brett forget that Leffertz was blind. His sight had been lost to shrapnel back during Desert Storm.

"That's only fair," Brett agreed.

"If you're sure I'm your man, then I'm stepping up," Levon sai● an● exten●e● a han●.

Brett took the rough, workman's han● in his own.

"Welcome to the team, Levon."

"What team, Brett?"

Gunny Leffertz' ●onkey-bray laugh fille● the room.

35

It was kind of fun when she forgot why they were camped up here in the woods.

Merry sat on a slanted stone and poked the embers of the dying campfire with a stick. Sparks rose into the cold air to join the stars in the night sky above. The occasional snuffle and huff came from the horses, which were dozing along a hitch line slung between trees farther up the hill. Jessie and the girls were asleep in the shelter of Uncle Fern's old still shack. The mossy roof was sagging over the corroded thumper inside, but its stone and log walls still blocked the wind.

Merry heard a brittle crunch of leaves behind her. She turned to see Jessie Hamer stepping from the still shack, shrugging into her coat as she walked.

"Couldn't sleep either?" the girl asked.

"I guess I got a thinking problem. You know that song?" Jessie said as she crouched to take a seat on a fallen log on the other side of the fire.

"I don't think so. Is it country?"

"Yeah. It's cute."

Rather than sit idle, Jessie snapped some kindling

and tossed it into the ring of river stone that surrounded the fire. Fresh flames consumed the twigs. Merry leaned over to place a pair of sawn branches atop the fire, and the glow sent their shadows flickering in the dark branches of the trees all around them. Merry moved an old speckled coffee pot to rest close to the fire.

"We can't stay up here forever," Jessie said.

"I know," Merry said. "My daddy only put enough stores up here for a month. He was a prepper when prepping wasn't cool." She was referring to the airtight drums hidden at the rear of the still shack and covered with a camo canvas tarp. They contained dehydrated meal packets, rain gear, blankets, a full medical kit, tools, and solar batteries. The spring farther up the hill provided fresh water for the production of the whiskey that had been made by five generations of Cades.

"You know what I mean, Merry."

Merry nodded with a wincing smile.

"I have a business. Clients. I can't put them off forever. Sandy's due at school. It's coming up on three days we've been up here. No one's come looking for us."

"And Uncle Fern."

Fern had called Merry on her cell to tell her that the walk-in clinic sent him to the urgent care center for his chest pains, and they had referred him to County Memorial, where they diagnosed him with gallstones and admitted him. He was due to be in surgery in the morning.

"He'll be okay. That tough old bird will come through fine, but he'll need you at home to look after him for a few weeks or so."

"So, you think we should ride back down?"

"Those men have no idea where you live. My truck is there now. I can work off of your property till the end of the week. Besides, I think they're long gone."

"You sure?" The coffee pot hissed and bubbled. Merry lifted it from the fire using a cloth wrapped around the handle. She poured them mugs of tea while Jessie spoke.

"I can't *know* that. But those buttheads were small-timers, I can tell you that. It makes no sense for them to keep after one little girl. It's not like that kind are afraid of the law, even if there was anything Esperanza could tell the police. Or if the police would even listen if she did tell them everything. And there's not a lot of cartel activity in the county these days. We both know why that is."

Merry nodded.

Her father had tangled with some criminals up from Mexico in these very woods a while back. As far as she knew, there were still bodies in the woods, or what was left after the coyotes got to them. As with most folks who messed with her daddy, the bad men had cut their losses and decided to move their business elsewhere.

Only the federal government showed the will to take on the Cades on any kind of persistent basis. The Treasury department had made it their mission to bring in Levon Cade to face their brand of justice. At least some of their agents did. For one in particular, it was some kind of sacred trust.

With her daddy overseas and out of their reach, they had turned to Merry, sending her into the tender mercies of the foster care system until a feisty child advocate out of Birmingham made them back off. But Merry knew they still wanted her daddy on a long string of charges, and he'd be in big trouble when he returned to Alabama.

And he *would* return. Merry Cade knew her father. Despite his sins, Jesus loved her daddy and would see him safely home.

"We'll ride down in the morning. Can you take me over to see Uncle Fern?" Merry asked.

"I sure will, honey." Jessie smiled through the steam rising off her mug. "This will all work out fine. You'll see."

* * *

"Oh, shit," Jessie Hamer said.

She stood at the Gas 'n' Go the next morning, holding in her hands the flyer she'd found taped to the side of the fuel pump. It featured the photo of a smiling Esperanza. A half-dozen of the phone number tabs had already been ripped from the bottom.

Jessie crumpled the paper in her fist and shoved it into the pocket of her barn coat. She turned back to see her daughter, Merry, and Esperanza talking in the cab of the truck. The stereo was turned up, sending a muted thump of bass through the rolled-up windows. None of them had noticed the flyer or her reading it.

The truck now gassed up, Jessie slid behind the wheel with a cheery smile fixed on her lips. She dialed down the radio volume to a whisper.

"Tell you what, Sandy. You can miss another day of school, right?"

Sandy strongly seconded that motion.

"We've been through a lot, and Merry needs our help. We'll all go visit her uncle together, okay?"

Along the county road to the Huntsville Highway exit, Jessie saw more flyers stapled to utility poles.

"Looks like someone lost a dog or something," Merry said.

"Looks like they really miss it. Hope they find it," Sandy added.

Jessie gunned up the ramp toward the highway, her mind weighing and rejecting options that grew in number with every mile south.

36

Gunny Leffertz said:
*"You're gonna go to bat for some assholes now an•
then."*

It was several days before Levon was outside his hut at
the same time as the men in Hut 2.

Security had been tightened following the double
murder in the shower building. For the time being,
showers were suspended entirely, and each hut was
taken for meals separately. This process took up most
of the morning and evening. They ate midday meals in
their cells, buckets with cheese and cold meat in rice
brought to them by unhappy, overworked kitchen
trustees.

There was no open exercise time either, which
caused more unrest than even the hurried meals and
lack of showers. Depriving these men of distraction
was a risky tactic. Taking away their football was
nothing short of madness. Fights inside the huts grew
more frequent as tempers grew short in the cramped
quarters with nothing to do but get on one another's

nerves.

The men in Levon's cell crowded at the window to take turns peeping through the gap in the shutters at the latest row. Levon took his turn to see guards dragging men from a hut on the other side of the broad lane. The Prick was there, giving his stick a workout on the backs of two men kneeling and hunched over on the gravel. He slammed the toe of his boot into each of their backsides, and one of them went sprawling, hands on his crotch. The Prick waved at the guards to haul them both away.

"Where are they taking them?" Levon turned from the window, the little Thai eager to take his place for a look.

"Inside the fence. The guard building," Klaus said, looking up from a chess game he was playing with the Japanese.

"What happens there?"

"They beat them some more. Maybe lock them up in the sponge room."

"What's the sponge room?"

"I have only heard it mentioned. Something unpleasant, I am led to believe." The German shrugged, gesturing with the butt of one of his last cigarettes.

* * *

Two days into the strict regimen, it was debatable who was sicker of it, the prisoners, or the guards.

The lockdown was called off, and they were soon back to regular meal rotations and outdoor exercise during daylight hours. Football resumed, along with the smuggling, pimping, payoffs, and other illicit activities barely hidden from plain view. Games and commerce rolled on, not the slightest bit discouraged by the intermittent cold drizzle from the overcast sky.

Levon stayed by the edge of the football pitch, seated on the wooden bench with a few other men. He feigned divided interest in the game and a paperback book with a garish cover showing a woman dressed only in leather chaps using a bullwhip to strangle an unshaven cowboy. It was in Greek, which he couldn't read.

He sat at the end of the bench, half-turned from the game play on the field. This allowed him a vantage point to watch the front of Hut 2 through a gap between two barracks buildings.

Levon knew what Mehmet Sadıkoğlu looked like without help from Klaus. His target was indeed a famous man in Turkey. Levon had been able to find photos of him in some of the Turkish language tabloids that were all over the camp.

Toward the end of the day's second game, Levon saw a trio of guards approach Hut 2. They undid the locks, and hammered on the wall with truncheons. Thirty or more men filed out from inside. Levon pocketed his paperback and made his way in an easy walk to the alley between the buildings that stood across from Number Two. Sadıkoğlu was harder to pick out of the group than Levon had anticipated. A number of the men had the same slight build, carefully trimmed beard, and wire eyeglasses that the journalist had in his photos.

It was the deference the other prisoners showed him that sorted Sadıkoğlu from the pack. He had gangsta cred in his own world that the others bowed to. He took up the lead spot in the march for the dining hall, a guard walking either side of him as escorts.

The man bore himself like the first among equals,

wearing his oppression as a badge of honor, a résumé enhancer. He was a prisoner, but a special one—a man who posed such danger to the people in power that he needed to be removed from society, but at the same time, kept safe from harm. There could be no risk taken of this man becoming a martyr. When the political winds blew the other way one day, he would be freed, and these days, having been a prisoner of the state would be a subject for dinner parties.

Levon broke into a trot and then an open run to intercept the head of the column of men. The guards were slow to react, perhaps thinking this sprinting man was chasing a runaway ball.

With his full weight behind it, he drove the heel of his hand up under the chin of the nearest guard. The man's feet left the ground and he went flying.

Even before that guard struck hard on his back, Levon had made a rigid claw of his left hand and driven the hard edge of his knuckles into the throat of the next guard.

He ripped the lead-weighted truncheon from the second guard's wrist with a snap of the leather thong that secured it there.

The third guard was charging for him, truncheon raised and shouting for backup. Levon struck him in the knee with his borrowed truncheon and laid him out with a tap behind the ear.

Through all this, Mehmet Sadıkoğlu looked on as a spectator the way the other prisoners did. It wasn't until Levon had yanked him close to put the smooth wood of the truncheon across his throat that he realized the guards were not the true target of the attack.

Pulling the smaller man before him in a chokehold, Levon backed between Huts 2 and 4. He gripped

LEVON'S TIME | 155

Sadıkoğlu firmly but not painfully. He could smell the fear coming off him. The man's hands slapped the air impotently. The other occupants of Hut 2 followed at a distance, but only to gawk.

Levon's mouth was close to the journalist's ear so as to be heard over the building roar of voices and whoop of sirens from the yard.

"Do you speak English?" Levon whispered.

The man nodded as much as Levon's hold would allow, his chin prodding the American's forearm.

"Someone wanted me to kill you. I'm warning you instead."

The gap between the buildings closed, with three guards parting the gawkers before spreading out to block the way. One of them was the guard he'd bull-rushed to the ground. There was blood in the man's teeth, and his face was a mask of bestial fury. Behind them, prisoners regathered to watch the show. Levon turned his head enough to see more guards behind him, preventing further retreat.

"What do you want from me?" the smaller man asked. His voice squeaked.

"You need to be isolation. Solitary." Levon relaxed his grip a bit.

"How do I do that?"

"We're going to fight the guards together."

"They will beat me."

"Not as bad as they're going to beat me." With that, Levon shoved Sadıkoğlu toward the guards in front of him.

The journalist made a half-hearted swipe at a guard before being shoved to the ground and kept there under a flurry of kicks.

With the same motion he used to fling the little

man away, Levon whirled, throwing the truncheon to crack off the skull of a charging guard. That man went down, unconscious, and two more guards stumbled over him. That gave Levon time to close the gap. He tackled a guard, lifting him bodily to use a ram on the phalanx that had filled the narrow alley. He fell in a scrum of kicking legs and swinging batons.

A sudden burning pain seared across his back to turn his vision red around the edges. He still gripped the guard he had tackled, and they shared the charge of the taser contacts now stuck to the back of Levon's damp coat.

Levon tumbled off the man to lie on his back. Hands shaking in an uncontrollable palsy, he could see the Prick approaching. There was a smile on the man's face. The Prick released his spent taser from his gloved hand to accept another one, fully charged, from a guard behind him. The man's thin smile broadened, showing tobacco-stained teeth as he straightened his arm. The guards around Levon backed away as the second taser was discharged, the contacts flying toward Levon on loops of thin cable.

The fire in his muscles was stoked higher. His back arched, his form rigid with pain. A barked command came through the drumbeat of his pulse—the Prick calling in the jackals.

Boots, fists, and truncheons rained down, barely felt through the electrical fire from the twin taser shots. He did his best to raise his arms to protect his head and curl his body to shield his guts and loins.

After a while, it didn't matter. The fire died away, and the light went with it.

37

Amalia was reminded of Kiko.

Kiko was a kitten, a little black kitten, she had found when she was a child. She had been maybe five or six years old. She found the tiny thing in the weeds behind the house she lived in with her father and mother and sisters and brothers. A house? More of a shack, a single room with stacked cinder block walls and an aluminum-sheet roof. Her father said it was all he could afford on his pay from working on the pipeline, but there was always money for beer and cigarettes. Always money for him to play cards.

She kept the kitten hidden in a shed that stood against the fence that surrounded her yard. At each meal, she would save a mouthful, spitting it into her hand once she was away from the others. She slipped back to the shed to feed the kitten. Kept a cracked saucer of water filled for the little one to drink.

At night, she prayed that Kiko would not cry out or scratch at the door. She prayed her father would not find Kiko.

Her prayers to God, Jesus, and the virgin Maria

bought Kiko five days.

Amalia's father came home late from the pipeline one night. He was drunk, but not insensate enough to miss the mews coming from inside the shed. Kiko came to him, hungry still, rubbing against the leg of his work pants.

He killed the kitten with a brick. Amalia found it the next morning before school. She dug a grave and marked it with flowering weeds. Her mother yelled at her because her hands and knees were dirty.

Amalia thought of Kiko now because of her new secret. The phone the boys had given her was something she had to keep from the eyes of everyone. Her children would ask too many questions. They would tell others, as children do. She would not tell her husband since she would have to explain it to him. It would not help his failing health to be worried over the threats the boys had made. She did not want him anxious that they were unsafe. He was not strong enough.

She swaddled the phone and charger in a towel to mute the occasional beeps it made. Amalia knew little of these phones. Some of the women at the sneaker plant owned them. She wished she'd been more curious, asked more questions. To be interested now might seem suspicious.

A few times it rang. She answered it each time, and each time, it was men speaking in Spanish or English. Always laughing. Always saying terrible things. Was this the world of Al-Obama? Was this where her little girl was now?

When it was safe, she would open the phone on her own. She understood enough to know that the tiny bar at the top corner of the screen represented the battery life. It was already nearly halfway down from when the boys had given it to her three days before. How could that be, from answering just a few calls? Perhaps opening it to check the screen used power.

She was so alone. Amalia wished she could share her secret with someone. Someone who might have an idea to help her. Or just someone to pray with, to tell her not to worry so. There was no one she trusted enough for that.

She worried that the phone might run out of power when she was at home and far from an electrical outlet. Amalia would have to recharge it at the plant. It was like a living thing, a thing to be guarded and fed.

Like Kiko.

And in one way, it *was* alive. It was a lifeline to her daughter. If it rang, it meant her little girl was alive. If it rang, it meant that Amalia would not have to repay the men who took Esperanza. If it rang, it meant Carlito would stay with the family.

She arrived at work early and made her way to her assigned station at a long row of women seated on stools and bent over machines to sew soles to sneakers. It was one of many rows under the fluorescent lights that hung from the ceiling of the cavernous room. The woman who worked her station overnight was still there. Today it was jogging shoes in a rainbow of colors on a pink rubber sole. The hundreds of machines created a random rhythm like rainfall on a metal roof. Cardboard cartons sat by each stool, loaded with finished sneakers.

A section supervisor stopped to speak to Amalia. He lifted one cup of his ear protectors and asked why she was so early. She explained that the walk was cooler before the sun rose. He nodded and moved on.

There was an open outlet under the lip of the worktable near her station. She eyed it with hungry eyes, imagining the little bar on the phone in her pocket shrinking and shrinking toward zero. Other workers from the day shift drifted in to help themselves to coffee or stand along the walls talking.

The klaxon sounded, and the women along the tables rose to leave. Amalia rushed in to take her stool. The woman at her station made a remark Amalia did not hear. Others laughed. She had seen this woman twice a day for the past five years, yet she did not know her name. She forced a smile for her departing co-worker before turning to her machine.

Before the rest of her shift could reach the table, she had the phone and charger out of her smock. She plugged the box in and rested the phone and cord on a ledge under the table. Her knee could touch the underside of the ledge. She hoped she would feel the vibration of it ringing through the metal surface.

The full cartons of completed joggers were taken away and replaced by empty cartons. Soles and shoe tops came down the conveyor that ran through the center of the long table. It would run all day at a crawl. Thousands of sneakers would be completed each day at this station alone, and tens of thousands more across the whole of the plant. Today was men's size seven. Smaller shoe. Less sewing. The supervisor would expect Amalia to fill two cartons before her ten-hour shift was done.

The mindless work went on, a set rhythm that would only be interrupted by the midday break for lunch and an evening break for dinner. The company provided the meals, but watched the workers carefully to make sure there was no pilfering. They had no interest in feeding anyone but the workers. It always made Amalia think of Kiko.

Somewhere in the world outside, the sun had come up. The fans above them whirled to life to add an ambient drone to the tap-tap-tap of the machines. She pressed her knee hard up on the ledge. She would never hear the phone over the din of the plant.

She left her station to line up for the midday meal. Each section was called in turn and given twenty minutes to eat a prepared sandwich or a bowl of rice and beans. Sometimes there was sliced oranges or mango. Everything was washed down with a watery fruit drink. They cleaned their hands afterward at a long trough and dried them on towels handed to them by an attendant. There was no time to wash their hands before they ate, but they were not allowed to return to work without doing so.

It was not until Amalia had received her paper-wrapped sandwich and drink that she realized she had forgotten the phone. She put her lunch down on a table and ran back to her station through a group of women from another section approaching for their own meal. She sprinted between the rows of long tables to see Señor Kim standing at her stool.

He was standing at her stool with the phone and charger in his hand.

She approached him, eyes lowered and offering apologies. He was scowling at her, displeased, scolding her in sing-song Spanish. This row and the one next to it was shut down for the midday meal. The machines were silent.

Silent enough for her to hear the insistent buzzing of the phone in Señor Kim's hand.

Without a conscious thought, she lunged forward

to grab the phone from her supervisor's hand. His face was a mask of outraged surprise, but Amalia didn't care. She ran from him, the phone open and pressed to her ear.

"*Esperanza? Mi niña! Mi niña!*"

38

Gunny Leffertz said:
"A goo♦ beating's like a goo♦ ♦runk. Only hurts the next morning."

He came around feeling pain in every joint and muscle. There was a copper taste in his mouth. He was naked, and his flesh was greasy with a sheen of sweat mixed with his own blood. He was seated in a straight-back chair, his wrists secured behind it and the chain looped through the slats. He kept his eyes closed and his ears open.

It was an enclosed room, deeper than it was wide, with a low ceiling. He could smell fresh tobacco smoke over a background scent of sweat and garlic. Urgent electronic voices issued from a speaker at the end of a room. When they were joined by a female voice, he opened one eye a crack.

A uniformed guard sat at the far end of the room, lounging back in a rolling office chair, his feet up on a desk. He was watching an obviously American television show dubbed in Turkish. A cop show. Two men in ties with guns and badges speaking to a woman in a low-cut blouse with an athletic body and a Botoxed face. There was a bank of surveillance monitors or rather, a bank where monitors should be. The recesses for the screens were cut in the facia board, but no electronics had been installed. The only screen was the one on the laptop.

All of the cameras across the camp were dummies. That explained why Levon wasn't suspected of the two killings in the shower building. He closed the eye again and feigned a sleep that became real.

A finger prodded his jaw. A man was speaking.

"Kukola? You want? Can have this."

Levon opened his eyes to the same guard he had seen watching TV earlier. The man was smiling and holding up a red and white can of Coca-Cola.

"Kukola? Is good?"

Levon nodded. The man popped the top and levered the can so Levon could slurp a few mouthfuls.

The metal door of the room banged open. The Prick entered and crossed the room in three strides to swipe the soda from the guard's hand with a swing of his rattan stick. A younger guard followed him and watched as the Prick dressed down the first guard in harsh terms. The kind guard, the good cop, was ordered from the room. The Prick closed the laptop with the tip of his stick and took a seat in the swivel chair.

"The commander will ask you questions through me. I speak English. Do you understand?" the younger guard asked. He had a touch of Cambridge in his adopted accent.

"Yeah, I understand." Levon's voice was a croak. He was dehydrated.

"Very good. Excellent." The younger guard turn to the Prick, who muttered a question for him to translate for the prisoner and then translate back. The exchange went on like this for a while.

"Why did you attack that man?"

"He reminded me of someone. Someone I don't like."

"But he is *not* this man, this man you dislike."

"I was mistaken."

"And this man you dislike is here? Is a prisoner?"

"No. He's probably back in Toronto. Fucker owes me money."

In response to the translated reply, the Prick waved the end of his stick at Levon, pointing there, there, and there.

"You have many scars."

"I get in a lot of fights."

"You are here for fighting. You like this fighting?"

"It's just something that seems to happen. Some guys get the girls. I get into fights."

"Some of these are bullet wounds."

"Sometimes it's those kind of fights."

The Prick's frown deepened. He growled further questions.

"This other man, the one you attacked, says he doesn't know you."

"I told you that. I don't know him. He doesn't know me. I just lost it. You know what 'lost it' means?"

"We think this story is a lie. You both are lying. We will hold you until the truth is told."

That meant they were keeping Sadıkoğlu in a cell in this building. He was safe for now. The truth would probably come out eventually, but not from Levon. He had no cause to trust anyone here. Not Sadıkoğlu.

Not the guards. And certainly not the Chechen. For all he knew, Levon was supposed to kill this journalist, then be killed himself. If Sadıkoğlu died at the hands of another prisoner, a Western-born one at that, the government's hands were clean. There was no other reason why a thug like the Chechen would want some anti-Erdoğan reporter dead. It was the scenario that made the most sense.

Levon kept playing dumb through another series of questions about past associations, his life in Saskatchewan, any contacts he made in prison, and anything he might wish to reveal about any illicit behavior in the huts. Levon played it straight and stupid, even faking passing out at one point to be brought around by a strop across the thigh from the Prick's baton.

The Prick circled behind Levon, out of his sight. He must have beckoned the young guard to join him. They had a conversation in low tones before the young man hurried from the room. The Prick remained behind Levon, rhythmically slapping his baton on the leather palm of his glove. He was playing the bad cop to the hilt.

The young guard returned with two more burly guards. One of them was the big guy Levon had used as a battering ram in the yard fight. The guy had a black welt under one eye. When they undid his cuffs and helped him stand, Levon feigned more weakness in his legs than he felt. They re-cuffed his hands before him and frog-marched him toward the exit. The young guard held the door open and asked a question.

"*Sünger o*•*ası,*" the Prick said.

The sponge room.

39

Gunny Leffertz said:
"It can always get worse."

They led Levon from the surveillance room down a corridor that ended in another steel door. Past this door was a concrete corridor lined with more steel doors. These had viewports in them at eye level. A row of plastic pails was lined up against one wall near a brass spigot.

Levon was uncuffed.

"Take a bucket. Fill it with water," the young guard said.

Levon did as he was told, placing the bucket under the spigot and turning the knob. He stopped to stick his face in the stream. It tasted of rust but was cold. He took long gulps until a slap to the back of his head made him straighten. The bucket filled to the brim. The guards motioned for him to walk down the corridor to where the young guard held a cell door open.

The cell was approximately eight feet wide and ten feet deep. The ceilings were ten feet high. A single bare bulb was set in a recessed grate at the middle of the ceiling. All four walls, the floor and the interior of the cell door were covered in a quilted material. The fabric was rough, and the stain of black mold clung to the folds and seams. It gave beneath Levon's feet as he entered.

A padded cell.

"Now you will take a shower," the young guard said from the doorway. The other guards stood. The one with the mouse under his eye smirked. He made a remark and his comrade hissed through yellowed teeth.

"I don't get it," Levon said.

"A shower. You will take a shower," the young guard said again. He mimed upending the bucket over his head.

Levon did as he was told, holding the bucket over his head and turning it over to douse him with cold water. The water puddled on the padding under his feet.

"Now the bucket is your toilet," the young guard said.

The door was secured shut, and the bolts shot closed. The bulb above went out, leaving Levon in darkness except for a bluish glow coming through the slotted viewport in the doorway.

He stepped from the spreading puddle that was soaking the padded floor. Moisture was pressed up through the fabric everywhere he placed a foot. This was the sponge room.

He moved to the rear corner of the room, where the floor was damp but not soaking wet. He planted his feet together and leaned back into the corner. This was all the comfort he was going to get, but comfort was way down on his list of priorities.

They were loath to risk killing a foreign national from a country friendly to their own. There'd be no more beatings, but that didn't mean they wouldn't fuck with him at every opportunity and make his life a misery until he either broke or they were satisfied that he understood his place in the order here. And his place was lower than whale shit.

He spent the next few hours weighing all possibilities open to him. He could escape. He saw two clear scenarios for that. One was a solid prospect, but would probably result in a few dead guards. The other was less certain, but there would be zero lethality. He would work on the problem and seek other solutions.

His other option was to wait them out. That was looking like the best one. His original plan remained in place, with this tangent of it an unforeseen hitch. The beating and his current situation might even be turned to his advantage. It was all tenable. All in flux. Good planning allowed for fuck-ups. He'd learned never to allow frustration to play a role in his operations. Shit happened, and you moved around it, under it, over it, or even embraced it. He was the snake in the Garden. He was the lion in the den. He wasn't imprisoned in here with them. They were imprisoned in here with him.

Satisfied that his way forward was solid for now, Levon controlled his breathing, sipping air and releasing it slowly, bringing down his heart and respiration rates. He willed the pain away from tensed muscles and made his body lighter and lighter until his mind was free and he walked across the floor of a leafy holler from his youth.

40

She began crying at the sound of her mother's voice. She covered her mouth with her hand. The house was quiet in the hours before dawn. Esperanza was in the kitchen. The hounds were asleep under the kitchen table. One rose to stand by her at the sink counter, tail wagging and head up for a pat.

"Esperanza, my child, my child!"

Esperanza leaned on the counter, her vision swimming, hot tears burning her eyes. She had lain awake all night after finding the crumpled notice with her picture on it. She had offered to take the trash to the can outside the barn. The notice lay atop the trash, the paper white in the moonlight. Unfolding it, she was shocked to see her younger self in her communion dress. She tore one of the tabs at the bottom of the paper free and stuck it in the pocket of the new jeans Señora Hamer bought for her in Huntsville after they had had visited the hospital.

After dinner, she pretended interest in a movie the others were watching. They put up sub-titles in Spanish, but she could not concentrate well enough to follow the story. Something silly about police and a beauty contest. In her country, the police were never something to be laughed at.

She lay in Merry's bed all night, thinking of the little slip of paper. Merry and Sandy finally drifted off in the sleeping bags that lay on the floor between the bed and the door. In bare feet, Esperanza crept between them to the closet, where she retrieved the phone number from her jeans pocket.

The hallway was dark except for a shimmering glow from the room of Merry's father. She peeped around the corner of the door and started. Señora Hamer was propped up in the bed, a tablet device leaning against a pillow in her lap pulsing with blue light. The white wires of earpieces looped to her head. From the regular rise of her chest and forward tilt of her head, Esperanza realized that the woman was asleep.

In the kitchen, she picked up the wall phone and listened to the dial tone before entering the thirteen-digit number. It rang and rang. She listened to the ocean noise between the rings, and imagined her mother and father in their tiny apartment. She imagined them around a table eating a meal with her brothers and sisters, maybe a breakfast of eggs fried with peppers. It was warm there, and the sun shone brightly through the windows.

A sharp click was followed by a buzz, and her ear filled with a metallic champing sound echoing with voices behind. Her mother's voice spoke her name and she cried.

41

"You know, I'm supposed to be retired," Gunny Leffertz said.

"Like you could retire." Levon scoffed.

"Nice to get a little something extra in my envelope now and then."

"That mean you're paying?"

They were sharing a tall pitcher of Coors at a table overlooking San Diego Bay, enjoying the greatest weather on God's green Earth. A dry, salty breeze moved the flags slung from the yachts moored in the marina. The cries of gulls wheeling high in the afternoon sky rang out. Mothballed warships were visible against the green of Coronado Island across the water.

"Don't know how much longer I can mother-hen you, Slick."

"I want to have at least one person I trust in the program."

"You don't like Brett?"

"I know my function here, Gunny. I signed the papers and made the pledge, but to guys like Brett and

Tobey, I'm a tool, to be set aside and forgotten when the job is done."

"How do you know I'm not the same?"

"Because you're a shitty liar."

Gunny brayed at that.

It was only at Levon's insistence that Leffertz was kept on as his mentor, guru, and spirit guide. The blind gunny was there as an advisor as Levon went through the brutal months of physical abuse and psychological challenges of BUDs training with the SEALs, sniper training at Pendleton, a punishing course in aikido and Krav Maga with masters of those forms, and a second run through SERE, this time as an observer, watching the process from the outside. He learned to strip, clean, and go lethal with every piece of ordnance currently in use by military units around the world. Demolitions experts both military and private sector showed him how to dismantle, disarm, and build improvised explosives. He learned the state of the science of electronic surveillance, and absorbed a working knowledge of a half-dozen languages common in the world's recurring trouble spots. Through it all, the gunny was by his side, coaching him toward excellence in every chosen specialty.

The only area of expertise that did not come organically to him was long-range sniping. Practically born with a rifle in his hands, Levon was deadly over open sights inside two hundred yards. Working through a scope came hard to him, however. He got the math and physics, but he'd learned too many bad habits hunting deer, varmints, and pheasants growing up in Alabama. He couldn't shake them while peeping through the reticle of a 30X scope. He was good—damned good—but not a natural talent.

Gunny excused it, saying Levon was a "hands-on soldier," an "Old Testament, eyeball-to-eyeball killer." The agency had plenty of snipers, but warrior adepts like Levon Cade were thin on the ground. His learning became mission-focused now, specifically fixated on a high-value Abu Sayyaf target in the Philippines. His baptism as a hunter/killer was days away.

"You need to let me go home to Mississippi, Slick. Joyce won't wait forever. Time for you to leave the nest and fly," Gunny said. He split the dregs of the pitcher between them, not spilling a drop.

"Like Icarus," Levon replied.

"Hope you do better than that shitbird."

"Fly or die."

"You'll do fine. I almost feel sorry for the assholes. You did a shitpile of hard work. You're ready for this."

"I guess this is graduation, huh? The only one watching my ass will be me."

"Just don't stay in it for too long, son. You do your part, then pass the baton. Don't let them use you up."

"When's enough enough, Gunny?"

"When you can't remember the face of the last man you killed."

Levon looked into the unseeing eyes of the man across the table from him.

"You really are a shitty liar, Gunny."

Gunny slammed a hand down on the tabletop and roared.

42

Gunny Leffertz said:
"The only thing you can plan on is things not going like you planne."*

Judging by his internal clock, three days had passed.

He was given one meal each day, a piece of crusty bread atop a scorched mash of rice, peas, and lamb, and a plastic mug of water. These were slid through a port at the bottom of the cell door. He broke the days up with an exercise routine and meditation.

Because of the limited caloric intake, he confined his exercise to mostly stretching. His main challenge was keeping warm. During the day, the cell was comfortably filled with a warm fug of damp air from the evaporating puddle in the center of the floor. At night, that turned to chill condensation. He kept moving through the night, pacing a tight circle around the room, stretching and doing presses against the padded walls. Through the day, he leaned or sat in the driest corner and transported his mind to other places and other tasks.

Levon gave himself a deadline. In five days, he

would act. Any longer in this environment would be a risk to his health. He did not want to start down a path where his fitness deteriorated because of inactivity and poor diet. The quality and safety of the food was a risk, and eventually, it would make him sick. A bout of dysentery would weaken him and complicate any escape plan.

And the room he was being held in was toxic. Prolonged exposure to the mold encrusted on the floor and walls was a serious health hazard. No telling what kind of bugs were in the food and water. A lung infection or gastrointestinal syndrome would be inevitable if he stayed here for more than a week.

On the fourth day, three guards came for him. He didn't resist as they secured his wrists behind his back with cuffs. They marched him to another windowless room, where they sat him in a steel chair at a table.

The young guard, the translator, was already in the room, seated opposite Levon. The Prick leaned against a wall behind him, smoking a cigarette. At the center of the table was a digital recording device.

Levon was asked to state his name and place of birth for the record. William Brett Hogue. Moosejaw, Saskatchewan. He was asked about his time in Syria and the cause of his arrest in Altınüzüm. The questions moved to his fight with Mehmet Sadıkoğlu. Now it was a fight rather than an assault.

"I don't know why I picked him out. I guess I'm going a little crazy in here. All I want is to talk to someone from the Canadian consulate and—"

The translator tapped the recorder and turned to look at the Prick. The Prick nodded. The recorder was tabbed on.

"You were saying?" the young guard asked

"I'm a foreign national being held incognito. My

country doesn't know I'm here."

"And you do not know who Mehmet Sadıkoğlu is. You were not told to attack him."

"I don't know the guy. Never knew his name. I *still* don't know who he is. I just picked him out to go ape-shit on."

"So, he was chosen at random?"

"Is this thing on?" Levon asked. "I said I don't know the guy. He doesn't mean shit to me. I just lost it."

"And there is no history between you?"

"Not until I took a swing at him."

"And the guards?"

"They were in my way."

The young guard turned to the Prick, who shrugged. The guard shut off the recorder and stood to speak to the Prick. After a brief exchange, the young guard picked up the recorder and left the room. The Prick took his seat, smearing his cigarette across the tabletop to put it out.

"You will be returned to your hut. Know that I will be keeping my eye on you," the Prick said in overly precise French.

"And will I be allowed to speak to someone from the consulate?"

"That is being arranged." The Prick fixed him with a stare. The guy was holding back, but his eyes betrayed his frustration. Events in his little kingdom had gotten out of his control and he hated it. By association, Levon was the focus of his fury. But as a foreign national, even one being held incognito, the Prick was afraid to spend that fury on him.

The door opened and two guards entered. One placed a stack of worn but clean clothing and a new pair of slippers on the table. The other undid Levon's cuffs. They all stood witness as Levon put on the underwear, string vest, flannel shirt, drawstring pants, and wool socks. None of the clothes were his size, but they fit well enough.

He was escorted from the admin building and released, blinking in the noon sun, into the prison yard.

Klaus was the first to greet him outside Hut 14.

"You are quite the hero now," the little German said, walking by Levon's side toward the shower building.

"How did that happen?"

"Word of your attack on Sadıkoğlu got out somehow. There have been news vans and reporters at the gate for two days now. A couple were even allowed inside to speak to him. He is being relocated to another prison."

That explained why they had recorded Levon's statements. He was on record as confessing that it was an isolated incident. He was no longer held secretly.

"One of them was a BBC reporter. Did he speak to you?" Klaus asked.

"No one spoke to me except the Prick. I've been in the hole for the last three days."

"The sponge room? What was it like?"

"Damp."

"Your people will come now. Someone from your embassy." They had come to the lavatory door.

"Guess I'd better get ready for that. I need a shit and a shower." Levon turned to the shower-house guard, who responded with a nod.

"This is good news, is it not?" Klaus' face betrayed his confusion.

"It complicates things." Levon banged the door open to enter, leaving the German standing alone.

43

Rolo Moreno slapped the phone from the whore's hand and backhanded her onto the floor before picking the phone up from the bed to answer it. He was naked and dripping from the shower. He looked at himself in the mirror as he spoke, the ink covering his lean body in every place but his face, the soles of his feet, the palms of his hands, and his ass. Skulls and bones and his favorite guns. A tiger battled an eagle on his chest. Across his back knelt a big-titty *bonita*, bare-assed in an Aztec headdress bursting with feathers. She held a human heart in hands dripping with bright red blood.

"Who was that?" the voice said on the other end asked.

"Some *puta*," Rolo said. "Who is this?"

"Honesto Camarillo."

"Do I know you?" Rolo prodded the whore's ass with a toe and motioned for her to get him a towel. He sat on the edge of the bed to light a smoke and listen to this *cabron*'s story.

"We know the same people. Charlie Ruiz gave me your number."

"You're friends with Charlie?"

"We have an understanding."

"*Sí. Sí. Claro.*" Rolo took a towel from the whore. Her face had become a clown mask, streaks of mascara running from her eyes. She was maybe sixteen. Early in the game for her. A year or more, and she would learn to take a beating with a smile.

"I need you to find a girl for me."

"I am not a pimp."

"A particular girl. She's run away, but I know where she is."

"So, go get her back."

The *viejo* on the other end sighed. "It's complicated. I need a hunter. Charlie says you're the best."

"Is someone holding her?"

"No, but she might be hard to reach."

"You have an address?"

"Yes, but I'm not sure it will be helpful."

"Is it on Google Maps? I can find it."

"Google Maps is not to be trusted." The *viejo* chuckled at a private joke.

"Tell me more," Rolo said and lay back on the bed to blow smoke at the popcorn ceiling. The whore was in the shower, washing off her jet-black tears.

* * *

Rolo found Jerry Ramos at the iHop. What kind of man ate pancakes in the middle of the day? Jerry looked up, mustache dripping syrup, as his partner slid into the booth across from him. They were a study in contrasts. Rolo, snake-hipped in a black rodeo shirt, skinny jeans, and lizard skin boots. Jerry, big-boned and rangy in baggy Levi's and a cotton work shirt, dusty chukkas on his feet. Rolo with his carefully trimmed goatee and bird-like moves and Jerry with his droopy red Zapata mustache and reptilian energy, only moving if he needed to.

They'd first partnered down in Medellin. They had been kids then, hungry and wild and willing to do anything for cash. When the opportunities dried up there, they moved north to Panama, and then Mexico. They had crossed the border in Arizona three years back, ready to do the jobs Americans wouldn't do. They never allied themselves, remaining fiercely independent and loyal only to one another.

Their only separation in all those years had been when Jerry did some time at *Topo Chico* until Rolo could work up the cash to pay for his release. That was how brothers rolled, although they weren't brothers, or even cousins. Not in any way. Rolo was dark and pure Indio. Jerry was half-Irish. One of the *jefes* down in Medellin had tagged them as "the Spic and the Mick."

"There's a job for us up in Alabama," Rolo said. He helped himself from the carafe of coffee.

"That's a long drive," Jerry remarked around a mouthful of double-blueberry flapjacks.

"Nothing for us here right now in J-ville." They'd been in Jacksonville since August, picking up a collection job here, a muscle job there. The last paying work they'd had was an arson job on a dry cleaner's plant. Since then they'd been drinking, sleeping, and fucking. Spending, not earning.

"What's the job?" Jerry said.

"A girl. A kid. A *plaza* up there paid for her and she's rabbited."

"We need to hunt for her, or do we know where she is?"

"Might be a little of both. She's in the mountains at

some fucker's house. Hillbilly shit."

"Like home," Jerry said, his mouth crooked.

"Yeah. Like home." Rolo returned the grin.

They'd both grown up in the foothills of the Andes that lined the Aburrá Valley. Rolo was one of eight children, and they all cut coca in the hidden clefts high above Caldas. Jerry's parents were schoolteachers in Envigado. Both boys had found themselves in Medellin after running away from their homes. Rolo, little more than an indentured servant, had fled the backbreaking labor at the start of the narco chain. Jerry wanted to be far from an abusive alcoholic father and aloof mother.

What brought them together was their ruthless determination not only to survive but to triumph. They backed away from no one, and took on work the other grasping young men blanched at. Their masters, the men in the expensive clothes and cars, saw the value in these boys and put guns in their hands.

To Rolo and Jerry, the Spic and the Mick, it was an adventure. They were *campañeros, hermanos,* like the partners in the movies and comic books. Riggs and Murtaugh. Batman and Robin. Tough *hombres* who inspired fear in the enemies of their masters. The lives and the pain of others meant nothing to them. Everyone else, the men they killed, the women they fucked, were extras in the movie of their lives.

At least, that was what it was like when they were young. They were in their forties now, and it was all just a job. They were every bit as dangerous as before, but maybe a bit slower, moving with determination rather than passion. And because of their reputation for success, guaranteed results, they could ask for more money now. That meant more downtime between jobs for *putas* and pancakes.

Rolo played with his phone, then held it up for Jerry to inspect. The image was a satellite shot, all green trees but for a string of white road to a small clearing at the foot of an incline. A few rooftops sat at the edges of the clearing.

"Nothing around there but trees and shit," Jerry said.

"That means we can make as much noise as we want," Rolo shot back.

"When do you want to leave?"

44

Gunny Leffertz said:
"A little chaos goes a long way."

The sun was low in the sky. Flurries of snow swirled in the air, and the dark-gray clouds building to the east promised more. Prisoners had lined up before the dining hall for their evening meal. The final football game was done, and the players trotted toward the showers.

Levon met the Chechen's entourage returning from the pitch. The big man with the little head, his nose still covered in a plaster splint, carried the cooler and the lawn chair. Ball Boy walked with the net bag of balls over his shoulder. Between them, the Chechen puffed on a black cigar, huddled under a stadium blanket, his fedora pulled low on his brow.

Ball Boy separated himself from the group to intercept Levon.

"He does not wish speak to you," Ball Boy said in his tortured French.

"It's you I wanted to talk to."

Ball Boy shifted the load of footballs on his shoulder and tilted his head to hear more.

"Sadıkoğlu is still here," Levon said, stepping close. "I can still get to him. But I need a blade."

"What is difference?" Ball Boy's fixed scowl weakened and his eyes narrowed.

"I need that phone your boss promised."

Ball Boy shrugged and dug into a pocket of his coat. He came out with the duct-taped hilt of a blade in the palm of his hand. The spade-shaped blade was a four-inch length of white metal honed to a ragged edge on either side. It looked to have been made from a piece cut from a bunk frame. Ball Boy stepped close to hide the handoff from prying eyes.

Levon took the blade's handle in his fist. At the same time, he reached out to grip Ball Boy by the back of the neck. His fingers closed hard on the man's nape, his thumb driven into the soft tissue of Ball Boy's throat.

With a single motion, he pulled the smaller man to him and drove the blade again and again into Ball Boy's chest just under where the ribs met. The first blow snapped the xyphoid process from the tip of the sternum.

The blade, not long enough to reach the heart, tore into vital vessels that fed that organ. Ball Boy sagged against him, seconds from cardiac arrest.

The net bag fell to the ground, spilling open to send dozens of footballs rolling over the yard. Idle prisoners chased them over the gravel, kicking and tossing the balls in an impromptu football melee.

The Chechen turned in response to the hoots and cries of the men kicking balls, *his* balls, along the lane between the huts. He failed to notice the humped figure of his man lying dead on the ground. Too late, he saw Levon striding toward him. The man's face was a mask, and his shirt was black with blood to the elbow. A dripping blade was held close by his side.

"Yuri!" he called the big man's name.

Yuri turned in time to meet Levon's first assault. The big man raised a hand to block the opening lunge, taking the point of the jagged spade deep in the palm of his hand. Levon drove his forehead into the already-ruined flesh of the bigger man's nose. The cartilage snapped anew, sending blood in a jet from under the bandages. Levon twisted the blade and yanked it from the flesh of the man's hand. The second knife thrust was deep into the flesh under the point of Yuri's jaw. This blow was delivered with Levon's full weight and carried both men to the ground.

Levon rolled off the big man's still body.

The yard was chaos now, prisoners fighting over the footballs while guards raced in to break up the scrums that were turning into fistfights. The loudspeaker squawked to life and screeched orders for the men to return to their huts immediately. A guard, racing to join the fray, tripped over Ball Boy's still form and went sprawling.

The Chechen was hobbling toward the safety of the crowd that was exiting the dining hall to watch or join the growing brawl in the main yard.

Levon caught up with him, clutching him close in a choke hold and at the same time driving the point of the blade into the top of the spine where it joins the skull. The Chechen went limp, limbs quivering as the last signals from his brain reached them. He followed his fedora to the ground.

The crowd of hooting and laughing prisoners grew silent and backed away from the bloody man now crouched over the Chechen, rifling his pockets. The Chechen had no friends here. His corpse, lying in a lake of blood spreading across the dirt, meant debts forgiven and obligations lifted. No one called out in alarm. The clutch of men closed back in to create a sheltering curtain around the murder they had just witnessed.

His fingers found the phone in the Chechen's coat pocket, an older Galaxy with the battery at half-charge. He pocketed it and parted the ring of men standing around him to run into the dining hall. The cook staff had joined the lookie-loos outside, leaving the kitchen unattended.

Levon vaulted a steam table to open the larder and pull out plastic jugs of vegetable oil. He used a carving knife to slash them open and threw them to the floor, where a shiny lake spread across. He turned on all the burners on the propane stove, then found a tin of stick matches by the steam tables and lit the end of a folded apron that he tossed on the floor. He was out the door while the spill of oil smoked and then ignited.

He ran through the chaos in the yard and had gotten halfway to the shower building when the flames reached the cloud of propane. All eyes, guards and their charges, turned as ten-foot gouts of flame exploded from the doors and windows. With a kettle-drum roll, the propane tanks ignited one after the other, sending an orange glow across the camp.

By that time, Levon was in the latrine and up into his hideout above the shower room.

He crouched on a beam and wiped the blood from his fingers to use the touch screen. He accessed the Vodaphone account and tabbed in an international number.

* * *

He was paying for the cake all over again.

Brett Tsukuda's oldest daughter had a birthday that day. Twelve years old. The big One-Two. They celebrated with dinner at Carrabba's and a monster birthday cake from Miller's. Brett had one too many pieces. On top of the pasta at dinner, it was way too much wheat gluten for this Japanese boy. The reflux roused him from a sound sleep.

While the rest of the family slept, he was down in the kitchen munching Gaviscon tablets and sipping ice water. He heard the phone ringing somewhere, never good news at—what was it?—four in the morning? Jesus. He recognized the ringtone. It was *that* phone. Where did he leave it?

He trotted to the laundry room and retrieved his agency phone from the pocket of the pants he'd worn to work that day.

"You've got Tsukuda," he said.

"Hold for Centcomm," a female voice replied.

Centcomm. Not good. He padded back to the family room to flick on the TV. A Tucker Carlson rerun was on Fox. On CNN was a panel on gender discrimination in the entertainment industry. Jesus, didn't the news channels have news anymore? A male voice came on the phone.

"Deputy Director Tsukuda? This is Colonel Tim Reese, Central Command, MacDill."

"How can I help you, Colonel?"

"We got a phone call to one of our classified contact numbers. An older one. The man on the other end mentioned your name and asked us to relay a series of texts that followed the call after he broke contact.

Your office referred us to you."

"Did caller give his own name?"

"He said his name was William Hogue, and he would be contacting you through the Canadian consulate in Ankara."

"I don't recall him. The Canadian consulate?"

"Yes, sir. He said you had a mutual acquaintance. Barry Saref?"

Abd al Bari Sarraf, late of ISIS. *Very* late, since a Tomahawk missile had decisively ended the mass murderer's career three weeks earlier in an attack signed off on by Brett himself.

"He also asked if you still liked coffee with your sugar."

"Holy shit."

"Then you know the caller?"

"I damn sure do. When did this come in?"

"Just after noon yesterday. We only found it twenty minutes ago."

"Damn. You relayed those texts to my section?"

"Already done, sir. Just letters and numbers."

"Delete them on your end. Forget this call. Forget William Hogue."

"Sorry for the wrong number, sir." The connection ended.

Brett ran from the family room, detouring through the kitchen to snap up the Gaviscon. He munched a fistful while he dressed in his closet, phone on speaker. His wife Tonya, still half-asleep, picked out a shirt and tie for him.

"I need a secure room. Who's on duty tonight? Highest clearance. Have them meet me there. Both of them. Isolate and lock down all communications to me from Centcomm this evening. It's to be marked classified, eyes only, me and the two on-duty officers joining me. Thank you, honey. No, that was for my wife. I'll be there in twenty." He signed off.

"Is this a national or international emergency, or some interagency bullshit?" his wife asked, pulling his collar to straighten it.

"Interagency bullshit," he said, plucking his car keys from a tray.

"You could have worn a sweatshirt and sneakers, then." She followed him to the front door in her slippers and robe. He shrugged into a woolen coat as he walked.

"Shirt and tie's good. It's gonna be a long day," he said, turning to peck her cheek before leaving the house.

A long fucking day, he thought as he tapped his Audi to life and crossed the snow-slick driveway in his flat-soled oxfords.

45

"Do we walk, or do we ride?" Jerry Ramos asked.

"They would hear us coming on that road," Rolo Moreno said.

"Then we walk."

They were parked on the narrow country road where a crushed stone driveway began. A rusty, battered mailbox sat atop a leaning post; CADE was neatly painted on the box in block letters. The sky was low, clouds touching the treetops. It was just past noon, but it looked like dusk.

Rolo pulled their truck, an F-150 stolen outside Macon, onto an apron of dried grass under the shelter of some beech trees. They got out, shrugging into heavy winter coats. The air was dry and cold, bitter after the muggy heat of the truck cab. The lenses of Rolo's Wayfarers misted over and he tossed them back onto the driver's seat.

Jerry pulled rifle cases onto the tailgate and unzipped them. One was a Savage bolt action in .308, the fat barrel of a heavy scope mounted atop it. The second rifle was a Marlin lever-action in .357. No scope.

Not their usual weapons of choice, but they were common enough hunting pieces. They'd draw no suspicion or notice this time of year, especially not in this part of the country. That would allow them to move in close and keep the gunplay to a minimum. Less risk to their quarry; that was key. The girl had to be returned unharmed, or they could kiss the five thousand dollar payday *a•ios, amigo.*

They turned toward a crunch of tires on the road behind them. A Tahoe with rust-rimmed wheel wells pulled to a stop on the roadway.

"You goin' for deer?" the driver called once he had his window down. Older guy with gray whiskers and a SKOAL cap with a curved bill.

"Just back from hunting." Jerry shrugged.

"No luck, huh?" The driver smiled, lower lip bulging with a bite of chaw.

"Guess not." Jerry shrugged again. He took lead. His English was fluent and his accent flat.

"Good thing, too. Repeater and bolt-action season ended a week ago. It's percussion now through Christmas."

"That so? We're from out of state."

"Saw the plates. Don't you Georgia boys wear orange vests? Warden sees you with those rifles and no license pins, he'll take a shit on you."

"Well then, I guess it's a good thing we didn't see any deer." Jerry left his rifle on the tailgate to walk toward the idling truck.

"Just taking your gun for a walk." The driver grinned and nodded.

"And my buddy in his city shoes. You know the best barbecue around here?" Jerry leaned, a grip on the bar of the outsized trailer mirror frame.

"Depends on which way you're headed from here," the driver said.

"It would depend on that."

Jerry leaned closer, sticking his hand, with the snubby revolver tight in his fist, deep into the driver's down vest below the man's armpit. Three trigger pulls, the explosions muffled by the thick fabric and padding. He yanked the door open to use his booted foot to roll the driver to the other side of the cab. The door open, he put the Tahoe in drive and aimed it toward the side of the road behind their truck. He drew the lever to neutral and stepped clear. The SUV rolled on through the brush and deeper into the trees, twigs and branches snapping until it came to rest out of sight.

The revolver was slick with blood and bits of down fluff stuck to it. The same with his gloved hand. Jerry winged the pistol into the woods in a high arc, then scooped up some leaves lying on the road and scrubbed his hands before wiping them on his jeans leg.

"We walk the woods or use the road?" Rolo asked. He stood with the lever-action balanced on one shoulder the way he'd seen Steve McQueen do in a movie.

"Woods," Jerry said. He picked up his Savage and raised the tailgate.

＊ ＊ ＊

"It's going to snow," Merry said. "I can smell it."

"You can smell snow?" Esperanza asked, eyes wide.

"Uh-huh."

They were booted and bundled and crossing from the house to the barn. Fella trotted with them. The hounds remained where they were, dozing in the warm kitchen.

"I have never seen snow," Esperanza stated.

"You'll be seeing a lot of it soon."

Merry opened the barn doors, then closed and bolted them behind her. Tricky Dick gamboled from his stall to give Esperanza a playful butt with his horns.

"You better let him out into the paddock or he'll drive us crazy," Merry said. She had Bravo's stall open and was slipping a bridle on him.

Esperanza went to the doors at the opposite end of the lane between the stalls. The goat skipped ahead of her. She unbolted the doors and swung them wide. Tricky Dick bounded and kicked his way across the grass. She leaned out to look at the sky, an open palm held upward to catch the first of the lacy flakes drifting down.

"It's snowing!" She ran back to where Merry had Bravo cross-reined in the middle of the aisle.

"We'll take a walk in it as soon as we're done here." Merry unfolded a horse blanket and draped it over Bravo's back. With Esperanza's help, they did the buckle tabs to secure it to the gelding's flanks and around the base of his neck.

"I will tell my mama about the snow the next time I talk to her," Esperanza said. Merry ran a comb through Bravo's mane to undo a snarl.

Merry looked over the horse's withers at the other girl's eyes, which were dancing with delight.

Through the front doors of the barn, they could hear the bray of the hounds in the yard.

46

Gunny Leffertz said:
"One thing about Cana♦ians. They fight as goo♦ on the san♦ as they ♦o on the ice."

Levon sat alone in the truth room.

The same room as before. Same table and chairs. They had secured him to the chair with two pairs of handcuffs linked from his wrists to the slats of the chair's back. Flex-ties strapped his ankles to the front chair legs. He was still clothed. His right shirtsleeve was stiff with dried blood.

He gave himself up after he made his call and texts. He'd smashed the phone to pieces and dropped it in the shitter. After that, he stepped out into the yard, hands up. The yard was empty of all but guards. The prisoners had been herded inside and locked in their huts. The only prisoners who remained were the three bodies lying on the cold ground, dusted white with snow. The firetrucks had long departed, except for a lone fireman hosing down the ashes. The skeletal remains of the dining hall was still smoking.

The fights between prisoners had turned into a battle with the guards trying to control them. Spilled blood and the dining hall ablaze were a green light for misrule. In any situation like this—men forced into one another's company for years at a time—nerves were rubbed raw and hatreds festered. Give them a moment where order slipped into anarchy, and that was the time when scores were settled. First with each other, and then with their keepers. It had taken more than an hour for the Prick to bring the place back to something like the status quo.

The beating they gave him was a nominal, workman-like affair. No one was going to mourn the Chechen and his goons. Some other player would rise to take their place in the illicit trades within the camp. The guards would continue to get their payoffs. And none of them ate at the dining hall anyway.

They left him in the chair all night. Through the door, he could hear ringing phones and the thump-thump of men running in boots.

* * *

"What am I looking at?" Brett Tsukuda asked. "What are these numbers?"

He sat across a conference table in a Level-Four secure room in the Back Nine, the section under his direction in the counter-terrorism division that dominated the west building at Langley. Seated across from him were his second in the Back Nine, Mark Neubauer, and Anita Sharpe, the division's resident savant on global financials.

Mark was a garden-variety agency wonk near the end of his thirty, loyal, hard-working, and with no life outside the agency. He had prison pallor, thinning hair, and a roll of fat around his middle. Too many breakroom donuts.

Anita was practically a child soldier, recruited out of the University of Chicago in her junior year when her facility at deciphering mass quantities of numbers was revealed. She was a runner, a ten-mile-a-day gal. The only cholesterol in her system was her massive, restless brain.

The table between them was covered in files stacked by subject, color tabbed and indexed. It was all paper in this room. All hard copies. No electronics ever on this sub-sub-basement level. Not even wristwatches. Everyone and anyone entering this floor was wanded and weighed on a scale going in and out. *Every*one and *any*one, and every officer obeyed the rules with the religious fervor of a zealous monk. After the first time anything got leaked from this level, the director promised there would be regular, and painful, cavity searches.

"The first row is a GPS position," Mark said. "It places the caller at Tekirdağ, a prison camp on the Black Sea coast of Turkey. An F-type prison under the General Directorate. Max security. A mix of violent felons and politicals."

"Lovely," Brett said. "And this bottom row of numbers?"

"The first row is a Swift code," Anita said. "The next two rows look to me to be account numbers."

"Bank accounts?"

"Presumably, almost certainly, given the transfer code at the top," Anita agreed.

"To what banks?"

"I have no way of knowing that," Anita said. "There's no branch or bank or country code in the account numbers. No prefix code."

"Maybe the sender didn't know them," Mark offered.

"Cade knows them. The man never forgets anything."

"Cade?" Anita asked. "My file says William Hogue."

"His name is Levon Cade. A former asset." Brett pushed a thick file across the table. It was secured with bands. Anita undid them and began leafing through the papers inside.

"These are all police reports. FBI. Treasury."

"The agency has no record of Cade. He worked for an unnamed unit that is no longer operative. That accounts for the delay in notification from CentComm."

"Why is he contacting us now?" Mark asked.

"He's letting us know he has cash, but not where it is," Brett said. "I'd say he's looking to buy something."

"A Get Out of Jail Free card?" Mark said.

Anita was silent, her nose in the papers before her, eyes scanning.

"More than that. Believe me, Cade could leave that camp anytime he wanted to. He wants more than his freedom, and is willing to pay for it."

Anita held up the stapled pages of a report and spoke. "It says here that Levon Cade/Mitchell Roeder/Oscar Bruckman may have access to foreign bank accounts registered under various aliases and holding companies to Courtland Blanco."

"That con artist guy?" Mark asked.

"Who's that report from?" Brett asked.

"Treasury."

"Active?"

"It's open, but no updates for the past three months."

"Who's the lead investigator on it?"

"Most of these are cosigned by the same agent. 'N. Valdez,'" Anita read from one of the papers.

"Let's talk to her," Brett said.

* * *

The van was cold, but not as cold as outside.

"It's your turn to scrape the ice off the window," Carl said from his chair at the bank of monitors.

She turned to look at the camera set up on a tripod and aimed out the panel in the rear door of the van. It was covered in a fresh skin of ice. Outside, the sleet had turned to a chilly drizzle. The coffee cup held in her mittened hands had gone cold. She couldn't feel the end of her nose.

"I thought it was Bruce's turn," she said. She nodded toward the man in the hooded parka, sound asleep and snoring up front in the passenger seat.

"You promised to trade with him if he brought back coffee."

"Cold coffee."

"A deal's a deal."

"Fucking guys." She pulled her scarf up over her head and exited the van, ice scraper in hand.

The van was parked on the third level of a parking garage near enough to the Mississippi to get a constant wind off the river. East St. Louis in winter was no one's idea of a primo posting, but that was the shit sandwich she was handed after a months-long, very costly investigation came to fuck-all when her subject vanished like a ghost. In addition, she'd given the department a black eye when she overstepped her authority by having her subject's minor daughter consigned to foster care in an attempt to leverage the asshole into breaking cover. That didn't happen. What did happen was, she ran into a little firecracker of a child advocate who had friends in Birmingham. Before it was over, a fucking Alabama senator was calling her supervisor. Now she was staking out a print shop suspected of running off queer twenties. They were following up on a tip that the counterfeiters were waiting for a shipment of a rag paper close enough to currency grade to pass easily even in an ATM.

She'd gone from rising star to pariah. Sure, they'd have accepted her resignation, but she had bills to pay, and more than that, couldn't imagine life without her T-badge and gun. So, it was a funny money unit or the marshals, and there was no way she was rolling with *those* cowboy motherfuckers.

Which left her scraping filthy ice off a filthier van in a sub-zero wind tunnel on a dreary day in the Heartland.

The cell in her coat buzzed and vibrated and she pulled it out to read the screen. A 204 area code. Washington. No name. She pulled a mitten off with her teeth and tapped to answer.

"Valdez."

47

Merry stifled a cry at the first gunshot. At the second, Fella was up, ears back and hair bristling down his spine. The third and fourth shots turned the hounds' howls to high, keening cries of pain. Bravo stamped in his traces, blowing and rumbling.

Esperanza backed toward the open doors at the rear of the barn. Fella bounded past her, out into the back paddock. The ridgeback turned out of sight on a trajectory toward the gunfire. Merry caught up with the other girl and gripped her arm. With a finger to her lips, Merry led Esperanza back to Bravo. Together, they undid the reins and led the animal toward the open doors and into the paddock.

A man's voice shouted, the sound echoing off the wooded slope that rose from the rear of the property. More gunfire followed.

At a run, the girls led Bravo toward the fence line. Sensing play, the goat skipped after them. The snow was falling heavily now, the grass already iced with fat flakes. A man's voice shouted again, and another answered. They could hear some of the words now.

They were in Spanish.

Working together, the girls hauled on the top rail of the fence to pull it free. It was wedged tightly in place. They had no tool to help loosen it, and couldn't risk the sound a mallet would make in any case. This was the only way out of the paddock with Bravo, and they would need his speed to see them clear.

From the far side of the barn, a man's voice rose in a wordless roar.

* * *

Rolo Moreno stood panting over the body of his *hermano*.

Jerry lay on the ground, his throat ripped open. He was no longer making bloody bubbles. A feathery snowflake drifted down to melt in the body heat that remained in his open eye.

Near him, the still form of the dog lay in a pool of blood, sending steam into the cold air. This dog was different than the others spread out on the ground before the house. This *chinga perro*, this demon hound, had rushed up low and silent. It had gone for Jerry like a torpedo and its jaws had clamped down on his crotch. The big man's knees went weak and he was down, screaming in rage and pain.

Rolo circled them, rifle raised. The dog was all over Jerry as the man tried to roll free of the snarling beast. They were too close together for a shot. Rolo spun the rifle to strike the dog's skull with the butt, but the bastard had snapped and nipped its way past Jerry's flailing hands to get a firm grip on his throat. The dog twisted clear with a wad of Jerry's flesh clamped in its fangs. Blood sprayed everywhere. Jerry made a strangled, gurgling cry, his legs kicking and his hands trembling.

Taking two steps forward to meet the dog head on, Rolo pumped the lever of his rifle to send fat rounds into its head and torso. The dog tumbled to the ground, where it lay still.

"*Mier•a. Mier•a. Mier•a,*" Rolo chanted under his breath, until it became an animal cry shrieked at the lowering sky.

* * *

They freed the top rail and set it aside to work at the second, middle rail. It was stuck fast, secured in place by time. The swollen wood was seated in the post like it would never budge.

To hell with the noise, Merry thought. She leaned on the next section and kicked at the rail end with the sole of her heavy boot. Three kicks and she felt some give, the tension broken. The two girls crouched, hands and arms wrapped around the rail to haul it free. Tricky Dick, tail twitching, watched from the center of the paddock.

An inch, then two inches, and it began to give. With one combined pull, it was free, and the end fell to the grass with a thump. Fingers laced together to form a stirrup, Merry helped Esperanza up onto Bravo's back. The girl sat up on the withers, leaning out to take the reins. With a grip on the bridle, Merry led Bravo forward to step over the remaining bottom rail and onto the swath of coarse cogon grass that grew right up to the tree line.

At a shout behind her, Merry turned.

A man was coming from around the corner of the barn, moving in a wobbling gait. Through the swirling fog of snow, she could see the black shape in his fist.

A long rifle. The man saw them and shouted again, breaking into a run.

There was no time. Merry released the bridle and drove a shoulder into Bravo's flank to urge him clear of the fence. With her open hand, she slapped him across the rump as hard as she could.

Esperanza let out a startled yip as the gelding exploded forward, hooves flying, into the trees. Tricky Dick cleared the bottom rail in a single leap and the goat bounded after the galloping horse with a bleat like a baby's cry.

Merry followed, sprinting full out, legs and arms pumping. The man's voice shouted a third time behind her.

At the trees, she jinked left, then heard the crack of a rifle and the whickering sound of a round striking branches. She was inside the tree line now, and jinked right, running hard along a ledge behind the boughs of the big pines that grew there. A second shot, a wild one striking high in the trees behind her. The sound of hooves was gone now. Esperanza and Bravo were high above the holler and out of sight.

With the dense row of pines between her and the shooter, Merry pelted straight up the slope, going for distance. She glanced one time behind her for any sign of the man.

All she saw, to her dismay, were her own tracks in the fresh snow.

48

They sent a car for her that took her to Scott AFB,
then put her on a noisy, bumpy C-12J for the flight
to Quantico. At least it was warm. A driver and SUV
were waiting for her on the runway with a box lunch
and actually hot coffee for the ride into DC. She had
finished the turkey club and waffle fries by the time
they hit the Beltway.

At Langley, a smiling Asian man in a suit and tie
met her at the middle of the eagle.

"Nancy Valdez? Brett Tsukuda. Ready to go into the
matrix?"

Anything to get out of Illinois, she thought.

"Lead the way, sir," she said.

He escorted her through each vetting process
as they made their way deeper into the maze of the
counter-terrorism division. By the time they reached
the Back Nine, she'd repeated and signed her name so
often it no longer sounded right to her. They'd taken
everything with a trace of metal from her: her phone,
watch, bracelet, earrings, and badge. She'd had the
sense to leave her sidearm in a lockbox back in the St.

Louis office. They took the badge that had brought her this far and hung a lanyard around her neck with a plastic tag that contained only a bar code.

"Hungry? Thirsty?" Brett asked as the elevator went down one level, then two, then three. How deep did this thing go?"

"Water would be fine. I've had enough coffee for now." It wasn't all caffeine. She felt a tingle like a low electrical charge was being run through her body. This was the Well of Secrets she was descending into. None of the significance was lost on her.

The elevator opened on a slab-walled corridor lined down one side with doors of gray-painted metal. Tiny cameras along the ceiling turned to follow her and the deputy director to the one open door in the hall. Inside was a well-lit, wood-paneled room with a broad conference table surrounded by leather-upholstered chairs with upright backs. The table was covered with neat stacks of files, tabbed and color-coded. On the opposite side of the table sat a doughy guy in glasses and a wiry brunette who didn't look old enough to buy cigarettes.

"Mark Neubauer and Anita Sharpe. This is Treasury Agent Nancy Valdez," the deputy director said, pulling a chair out for Nancy.

"We're hoping you can match these numbers to accounts," Anita explained, standing to reach across the table with an open folder. All business.

"Thank you," Nancy replied. The DD had put a cold bottle of Fiji before her. One of the panels in the wall had revealed a well-stocked fridge. That unlimited, unaudited War on Terror budget was a trip, wasn't it?

Anita continued, "We have Swift codes and account numbers without prefixes. There's also what look like passcodes to those accounts, but we don't have bank names or country codes. Nothing to allow us to make a match, look into those accounts, or even verify that they're legitimate."

"This relates to a case I worked on?" Nancy asked.

"It does," Mark confirmed.

"Which one? I mean, I assume you're looking for my insight on this? I can't help you without more specifics."

Mark and Anita turned to Brett Tsukuda, who was standing at the end of the table.

"Levon Cade," he stated.

"Fuck me," Nancy exclaimed.

They handed her a file containing copies of her case reports as well as FBI, IRS, and DHS files relating to Corey Blanco going back ten years. So much for the ban on agencies sharing departmental classified material with one another. There were even copies of her handwritten case notes, along with every email and text that related to the subject at hand: Roeder/Brockman/Cade.

Blanco had been a swindler who preyed on billionaires. He was one of the rare smart ones who got out when the getting was good. He went from a celebrity moneymaker, as well known in Hollywood as on Wall Street, to a shadow figure living off his ill-gotten fortune in mansions placed in countries with no extradition treaties. His past caught up with him when he was finally successfully stalked and tortured to death by a gang of international hoods whose origins remained a mystery. Although they had gotten their man, Blanco had died before he could reveal the location of the Holy Grail, the Big Enchilada of his criminal venture, the key that would unlock all the places he'd hidden his loot.

That had led the gang on a world tour of Blanco holdings across five continents. The hunt had ended at a mansion on a remote lake in northern Maine, where the irresistible force of the home invaders had run into the unmovable wall of Levon Cade. Cade and his young daughter had fled Maine, leaving every member of the gang dead behind them. That started a multi-state crime spree ending in the hills of Alabama just below the Tennessee border with nearly every local, state, and federal law enforcement agency looking for the father and daughter.

It had been long theorized that Cade had financed his run with cash funds taken from the vault back at Blanco's Maine hideaway. It was further conjectured that Cade might have gotten away with the MacGuffin the gang was looking for: the location, account numbers, and passcodes to the hidden Blanco fortune. The sum was estimated in the billions and much desired by many, including Uncle Sam, who wanted his piece. And by "piece," Uncle Sammy meant the whole damned pie. In whatever form Cade might be holding that list, on a flash drive, disc, or written in blood on parchment, these numbers he had texted were proof of its existence.

"Cade wants something in exchange for this," Nancy said. "What is it?"

"He hasn't said," Brett answered.

"Do you have him in custody?" Nancy asked.

"No. But we know where he is."

"Then you're in contact."

"Not at the moment. We're working on that," Brett told her.

She was able to make fairly educated guesses as to

the two accounts the numbers matched. The Swift codes helped narrow down the countries. One was a private bank in Antigua, the other in Taiwan.

"Try this one first," Nancy suggested. She slid a written slip of paper across the table. "The Eastern Caribbean Central Bank in Barbuda. It's one we suspected Blanco of using."

"You're one hundred percent on this?" Anita asked.

"Not one hundred, but it will let you enter the passcode twice before shutting you down. If you fail there, use the same number and code here." She tapped a nail next to where she'd written Caribe Banque of Antigua.

Anita took the slip of paper and folded it.

"I'm taking this upstairs to run it," she said, and rose to head for the door.

"Anita?" Mark called, half-rising from his chair.

"I'll bring back lunch," Anita assured him and was gone.

"Let me try to work out this second account by the time she gets back," Nancy said and ran a finger down columns of printout, with Brett hovering over her shoulder.

"What do you think we'll find here? In Blanco's offshores?" Brett asked.

"It'll be in the billions, minus what Cade spent."

"How many billions? Tens of billions?"

"Hundreds of billions." Nancy turned in her chair to look Brett in the eyes. "Corey Blanco was like a dozen Bernie Madoffs. He had ins everywhere. Silicon Valley. Big oil. Big pharma. Hollywood. Eurotech. They all wanted to play with the Magic Man. Now all that's in the hands of Cade, and he's using it to bail his ass out of everything from Murder One to felony assault to grand theft, and God knows what else."

"And these numbers could be proof that he has the keys to Blanco's kingdom?"

"Has it ever occurred to you that Cade might have been in with that gang? He could have been part of the home invasion, then decided to kill the others and keep the loot for himself?"

"That's a reach, Valdez. A big one. There's nothing in your own investigation to indicate that. Cade had been in place in Maine for months, over a year, before this treasure hunt kicked off in Costa Rica. With his daughter. There's no Venn diagram you can draw that brings him into the orbit of the crew that hit Blanco. And he'd have worked out a better escape plan than shooting his way home."

"Maybe he's just not that smart."

"You think Cade is some dumb hick," Brett stated. "You're pissed because he's been two steps ahead of you at every step."

"I say you let him stay wherever he is. I say you tell him to go fuck himself."

"Time means nothing to Cade. Deprivation and suffering? He'll stand up to it. And believe me when I tell you, he won't stay put where he is right now. It's hard to beat a man with nothing to lose."

"You're telling me he doesn't care about anything? Not even his daughter?"

"I read the files. You tried using her as a wedge. How far did that get you? The kid's as tough as the old man, and he's as tough as they come."

"Just another meathead you brainiacs raised like a veal calf to be a killer for you," Nancy said and turned her eyes back to the printout.

Brett took a seat across from her and leaned close.

At the far end of the table, Mark pretended to be consumed by the background files he had in front of him.

"You think he's some hick who managed to shut you down out of pure orneriness and dumb luck? Cade may talk 'bama, but there's an intellect there like I've never encountered before. If he were ever to consider keeping his ass out of trouble for five minutes, he could be anything he set his mind to. And whether we cut a deal with him or not, he'll be back in the States for sure, and not real pleased with what's been going on with his kid all this time. Personally, I'd rather have him back here on a friendly basis. The alternative is Conan the Barbarian, with billions in cash to weaponize."

"So, he's a danger to his country? An enemy of the State?" Nancy's brows knitted. She didn't have any patience for cloak-and-dagger elitist black-bag bullshit, all that "I'd love to tell you but then I'd have to kill you" crap she'd been hearing from the alphabet agencies since her first day inside the Beltway. And she was smelling it all over Brett Tsukuda.

"He might not feel real kindly toward some of its citizens. Look, Cade is an asset. *Was* an asset. Pure and simple. And I know he's a dangerous man. As recently as two weeks ago, he did a solid for this agency and his country, and do you know why he did that?"

Nancy waited, unblinking, for an answer.

"Because of a promise he made to a friend ten years ago. Now, as naïve as this may sound to you, I think we owe it to this guy to wipe the slate clean. He's paid for that in blood. Now he wants to back it up with cash. And *that's* something I can sell to my bosses."

"So, find you the money," Nancy said.

"Find me the money," Brett agreed.

49

She weighed her options and her challenges as she continued up the slope. She dragged a broken pine bough behind her to make her footprints harder to see. The trick wouldn't fool someone already on her tail, but it could mask her marks from anyone looking to cross her back trail.

The snow had stopped falling and the temperature had dropped. There was a half-inch layer over everything. The sun was already down behind the hills to the north. The forest was shadowed in gray gloom. Merry was in layered clothing that was enough for her trip to the barn to clean stalls, but not enough for an overnight stay in woods. The only way to stay warm was to keep moving.

Her other concern was Esperanza out there in country unknown to her. Bravo would carry her away, but the gelding would eventually give in to habit as he got hungry. He would turn back toward the barn. The men looking for her, some of them or one of them, would be waiting there for her.

How had they known to come here? She thought

back to Esperanza's words just before they had heard the first gunshots. She'd said that she couldn't wait to tell her mother about the snow. How would she do that? Something about the way she had said it tickled the back of Merry's memory. Something that made her think that maybe the girl had spoken to her mother recently. How was that possible? Had she spoken to her mother in Guatemala somehow? That would mean her own mother had betrayed her to the men who were hunting them now.

Merry came to the fire road that curved along the mountain face and dropped down to cross the watershed. She was five miles above Uncle Fern's land now. If she could climb higher, she would get a view of the long trail that looped back toward the farm. There was a section to the west that crossed a pocket clearing where the ground formed a shelf above the watershed. The path Bravo had taken off on would take him and Esperanza across it. The horse would follow that trail because it was familiar. Merry would have to find a way to warn them off.

Backing across the fire road, Merry used the length of pine bough to brush her boot tracks away. The snow looked disturbed, but there were no discernible tread marks.

The trees gave way to rockier ground above the fire road. There was a shelf that followed the road below as it snaked along, tracking along the natural grade of the slope. The snow turned the roadway into a ribbon of white. As she hiked, or rather, leapt from rock to rock, Merry kept her eyes to the road's surface as well as the rocks below her. The layer of snow could hide fissures in the massive slabs of stone. It would be easy to miss one and take a bad step that would leave her with a snapped ankle.

Another mile along, she came to a sharp turn in the road where it made its way around a promontory of boulders with a crown of scrub pine growing about its base. She stepped out onto the big caprock to look down on the curved section of road that was invisible from the shelf above.

She looked to the west, where the fire road dropped down toward the watershed. The clearing where the long trail looped south was out of sight past the bare branches of the birches that covered the shed land. Squinting to study the road ahead, she could see black marks in the snow. She moved closer over the rounded rock, stepping across a deep fissure in the stone.

The marks in the snow were from the hooves of a horse. Black against white, as clear as words on a page. The story they told was easy to read, too. The prints came onto the road and followed it west a bit to a place where it looked like Esperanza had reined Bravo in. There was a circle of impressions where she had tried to turn his head, but the gelding wasn't having it. He knew right where he was from the countless times Merry had ridden him in this same part of the forest. His head would turn toward the long trail where it passed through the sweetgrass clearing. In the end, the larger animal had won, and the hoofprints continued along the road until they were out of sight in the deeper dark.

There was no hope of catching up to them before full dark. Or before Bravo took them both back to his stall.

She wished she'd worn warmer clothing. She wished that Clif Bar that had been in her vest pocket yesterday was still there. She wished she could wet her dry mouth with some snow, but she knew the dangers of that. She wished her father was here. She thanked Jesus that her Uncle Fern was not. He'd be as dead as she was sure his beloved hounds were right now.

Then she shoved all the wishes and prayers and fears down deep to deal with what was happening now. Right now. Right here. That was all that mattered. Not what could *not* be. She had to think ahead to what might happen when she reached the farm.

They'd most probably have cut the phone lines. The electric, too. They wouldn't know where her father had hidden guns and ammo in the house and the barn and up on the eaves of the carport. The feds hadn't found them, and they'd spent weeks on the farm. And what if those guns *were* there, and she could reach them? She was no soldier, no hardass Marine like her daddy. She was familiar and comfortable with the rifles and shotguns that were kept handy or hidden around the property. Her daddy had taken her to the shooting range dug out of a hillside at the rear of the farm. The summer before, they'd fired thousands of rounds under her father's supervision and tutelage. He had told her she had a good eye, but needed to work on her breathing for long-range targets.

That would mean nothing against the kind of rough men who had come to the farm. These men were killers, and she'd seen their kind before up close. Way too close. She had no cowgirl fantasies that she could take on who-knew-how-many criminals and still be standing when the smoke cleared. This wasn't *Home Alone,* and these weren't the Wet Bandits.

Merry slid to a lower grouping of stones to make her way down to the road. She had no idea what to do beyond trying to reach the farm before Esperanza, but there was the long run down the mountain, and time to think of something that would save the girl from the men who had come for her.

She crouched to lower her foot to the next ledge beneath her when she heard the sound. A motor. A car or truck engine, coming from the east, its source still invisible around the turn in the fire road.

50

Rolo drove the F-150 at a crawl along the switchback road. The rifle was propped against the dash. His nine mil auto rested atop the console at his side. His eyes scanned the white surface before him, looking for any signs of disturbance. He got out a few times to inspect tracks that he recognized as deer.

As the sun traversed the peak above and threw the valley into shadow, he switched on his headlights. They helped him to see the road, but blinded him to all other surroundings. His world was reduced to twin cones of light. The white road in front of the truck ran under an arch of ice-rimed tree branches that looked like strands of crystal.

The road curved and recoiled back on itself as it followed the path of least resistance around the rim of the mountainside. It was seldom a straight run, and then usually less than fifty meters before the next right-hand turn.

Ahead of him, a great brow of rock jutted off the incline, causing the road to make a sharp hairpin to clear the point. The boulder angled out over the road, with only a few feet of clearance above the truck's cab on the right-hand side. He steered well clear of it, the twin beams of his brights sweeping through the trees to return to the smooth white surface of the road.

Something ahead threw shadows across the snow. The crust was broken in spots. Even moving at his snail's pace, the Ford slewed to a stop. The road surface was turning to ice under the fresh fall. He righted the truck to aim the lights down the road ahead.

He got out of the cab with the rifle in his hands. Rolo walked down the beams, his shadow stretched before him. The light pulsed with the rhythm of the Ford's engine. He came to where the snow was disturbed and crouched to take a look. Hoof prints, and recent ones. There was no snow in the prints. The girl on the brown mount had passed this way since the snow stopped falling. He walked farther, past where the U-shaped impressions first appeared.

The prints continued on down the road as far as he could see. She had come this way and was not far ahead of him. The horse would be blown after racing up the steep grade to this point. He would catch up to her easily. Then she would pay for Jerry, that horrible death. Mauled by an animal. His eyes had pleaded with his *hermano,* and Rolo had stood by helplessly. He couldn't kill her—there was no payday in that—but her owners wouldn't mind if she came back a little soiled.

Rolo was turning back to the rising glare of the truck when he heard the crunch of tires on frost. At first, he thought he had perhaps left the Ford in gear, and it was rolling on its own. Then the engine gunned with a throaty rumble, and the lights grew bigger and brighter. Someone was at the wheel. He turned to run from the road, slick soles slipping on the pebbly surface of the hardened snow.

The right front fender struck him hard in the side and he was airborne, tumbling into the icy blades of the ferns that sprouted along the roadside. He kept hold of the rifle even as he rolled to a stop, the wind driven from him. The truck slid to a halt, angled across the road. The twin orbs of the reverse lights flashed on, and the wheels of the Ford spun in the crust with a rasping sound.

Rolo tried to rise so he could hobble into the trees, but he couldn't. Pain lanced up from where the ball joint at the top of his left leg had become dislocated, a hairline fracture across the neck of the joint. He sucked in air, but one of his lungs would not fill, and the pain made him cry out. He fell back into the ferns, with only enough strength to raise the Marlin with one hand for a wild shot. One final act of defiance as the truck roared up on him and over his legs. The double back tires crushed his shin bones under their grinding weight. He dropped back to the ground, not enough air in his lungs to scream.

The Ford lumbered from the ditch to come to a juddering stop on the road. He raised his head to blink into the glare of the remaining headlights. The light on the passenger side was out, bashed in where the truck had struck him the first time.

A footfall broke the brittle layer of frozen snow near him. He reached a hand for the rifle, fingers splayed. A weight came down on his wrist, a booted foot. He turned his head, his vision red at the edges. A girl. The Anglo girl who had run from the barn. She held his own *pistolo* in her gloved hands, the black eye staring at him. The girl's face was pale in the electric glare. Her eyes were as dead as the pistol's.

"You were gonna shoot me?" she asked. Her voice quavered a bit, from the cold or the rush.

"That is the understanding we share," Rolo said. His voice sounded far away to him.

"You're gonna die out here. No one will ever find you." The girl stooped now to pick up the Marlin. All the while, his pistol remained trained on him. She stood, the lever-action balanced in the crook of her arm.

"So, what must I do?" His voice a dry croak.

"You don't have to do anything."

She turned and walked back into the lights. He heard the truck door creak, then slam. The beam of light retreated, then turned away. The truck was gone, and the night went black.

Then he died. And no one ever found him.

51

The men who came for him the next morning were military, Turkish army in forest-green camos and black berets. All business. Nothing was said but for *soto voce* directions from an officer in command of the four-man detail.

They undid Levon's cuffs and escorted him to the guard's shower room, where they stood outside while he took a long, hot shower. The dried blood came off his skin and out of his beard and scalp to make a muddy swirl around the drain.

Other soldiers were here. The Prick and his guard staff were gone. The blue uniforms were gone. Everyone was in forest camo. The surveillance room was open, and techs were busy running wires to brand-new monitors. The floor was littered with cartons and foam packing.

Clean clothes were waiting for him in a folded stack. Cotton shirt and drawstring pants. New socks and slippers. An olive-drab pullover.

They walked him from the showers to a break room, where a covered tray was brought to him. The steel mess tray was piled with scrambled eggs fried with chunks of *sukuk* sausage chopped into them, fresh bread, butter, and a pot of strong, eye-opening coffee.

When he was done, the soldiers took him to the interrogation room. A man waited in the room for him, seated with an open folder of papers before him. The friendly man had a broad, open face and a receding hairline. He wore a tie and a cardigan sweater. A can of Coke was open by his hand. He stood to shake Levon's hand. They took seats opposite one another and the soldiers left the room, closing the door after them.

"My name is Hank Ferlach, and I'm from the consulate. So, what part of Canada are you from?"

* * *

"One hundred and five, almost one hundred and six million." Brett Tsukuda was breathless from his run down the hallway to the secure room.

"The account is righteous, then," Nancy Valdez said. "And the US government can make a claim on it."

"That means this one is probably good as well." Anita Sharpe held up a piece of paper with the prefix code for the Taipei Monetary Exchange Bank.

"That also means we can break for lunch," Mark Neubauer said.

* * *

"You're *not* from Canada, then?" Hank Ferlach asked. His hand was poised, pen ready, but he was uncertain how to fill out the forms he'd brought with him.

"United States. I have my reasons for not wanting that known," Levon explained.

"If nothing else, your accent confirms that," Hank agreed. His smile was become fragile at the edges. "Now, why didn't you ask to contact your *own* consulate?"

"Because if I had to rely on my State Department, I'd be sitting here until I died."

"Well, I'm not certain what I can do for you, Mr. Hogue, with you not being a Canadian citizen and all."

"Do you have a phone?"

"I'm not sure…"

"Do you know what I did to get you here?"

Hank's smile melted away all together.

"Excuse me?" he asked.

"What did you see when you got here, Hank?"

"Well, the military seems to be in charge. It appears there were some murders, and apparently, a rather significant fire, followed by a riot."

"Do you have a phone, sir?"

Hank dug his iPhone 8 from his sweater pocket and placed it in the middle of the table.

Levon tapped the phone option and keyed in a number.

* * *

"You walk in here and take a big, greasy dump on my desk, and tell me it's a *goo⸱* thing?" the director asked from behind his glass-topped, *un*shat-upon desk.

"I'm just saying that there's an upside," Brett Tsukuda replied, standing where he could look past the director to the gray Potomac drifting by on the other side of the GW Parkway through the quadruple-thick ballistic glass.

"Are you talking about the money? This man is extorting the United States government, and you see that as a positive?" The director unwrapped a cough drop taken from a cut-crystal bowl and popped it into his mouth.

"Not quite extortion. He's going to *give* us money."

"In exchange for what, exactly?"

"His freedom and a return home with total immunity. A pardon, in effect. His record expunged."

"A *Presidential* pardon? That's impossible. And do you have any idea of the political capital it would require, the levers that would need to be pulled, to spring this guy from a Turkish prison? You've read the situation reports on our relationship with Ankara."

"If we don't free him, he'll free himself, sir. He'll be in the wild, and we'll have no leverage with him."

The director released a deep, mentholated sigh.

"What kind of money are we talking about here?" the director asked.

"If he's to be believed, and he has no reason to lie, we're looking at close to one hundred billion dollars in cash, metals, and other assets. In addition, he has intel on Corey Blanco's former associates that could lead to a potential Aladdin's cave of hidden loot. It's a criminal network with links to terror organizations. We're talking state sponsors here, sir."

"The pardon is out of the question. The President would never go for it. I'd advise him not to myself."

"A stealth pardon. We've done them before. Nothing official. Nothing on paper."

"He would trust us to keep our word?"

"Oh, *fuck,* no!" Brett laughed with a sudden honk, then recovered. "Sorry, sir. He'll have some kind of deadman switch set up if we screw him over. He learned from the best. Hell, he was *born* in a place where feuds are a real thing. He lives by a code."

"A code?" The director snorted. "What code?"

"As he put it to me, 'I don't get mad, I get even.'"

The director unwrapped another cough drop, then

squirted a spray from a squeeze bottle up each nostril. He wiped his nose with a Kleenex from a carved wooden tissue box. He slumped back in his chair and made a propeller noise with his lips.

"Take a walk, Brett," he directed at last.

"Sir, there's a timetable here..." Brett began.

"I'm going to call the President, and I don't want you to hear what I'm going to say to *him,* or the names he's going to call *me*." The director made a shooing motion. "Take a walk. Karen will buzz you when you can come back in."

"Thank you, sir."

"Fuck you, Brett."

52

He walked through a man door in the gate out onto a sidewalk that passed a row of mothballed Vietnam-era jet fighters. A blue Air Force gear bag was slung over one shoulder. He breathed deep and took in the smell of home.

She knew him by his walk. His shaved head and the bushy beard didn't throw her. He was thinner than she'd ever seen him, but she still knew him. She would know him anywhere.

Merry ran from the visitors' lot toward the main gate at Arnold AFB to leap at Levon. He caught her in his arms and crushed her to him. She spoke, her voice muffled against the shoulder of his coat. His neck was damp with her tears as he carried her to the waiting truck where Jessie Hamer and her daughter stood, smiling. With his free arm, he embraced Jessie as well. Sandy stood by, eyes gleaming.

"I'm home. For good. I'm never leaving again," he stated. Merry's hold on him tightened.

The rear door of the crew cab opened and a dark-haired girl stepped out, smiling shyly.

"And who's this?" Levon asked.

"That's Hope, Daddy," Merry said, smiling through her tears. "Her name is Hope."

53

SUSPICION OF ARSON IN FIRE AT AREA
BUSINESS

*Birmingham. Investigators from state CID have
release• a statement of their intent to look into a
suspicious fire at Dixi-Pro Lt• in Fulton•ale late
We•nes•ay night.*

*"There's evi•ence that this fire was helpe•
along," accor•ing to the press release referring to
the three-alarm blaze that •estroye• a permanent
structure along with a trailer an• several vehicles.*

*Local fire •epartment officials cre•it an
anonymous phone call that alerte• them to the fire
an• allowe• them time to contain it before it sprea•
to surroun•ing properties inclu•ing a lo•ge for
the Fulton•ale chapter of the Veterans of Foreign
Wars.*

*Efforts to locate the owners of Dixie-Pro have
faile•.*

SUSPICION OF ARSON IN FIRE AT AREA BUSINESS

Birmingham. Investigators from state CID have released a statement of their intent to look into a suspicious fire at Dixie-Pro Ltd in Fultondale late Wednesday night.

"There's evidence that this fire was helped along," according to the press release referring to the three-alarm blaze that destroyed a permanent structure along with a trailer and several vehicles.

Local fire department officials credit an anonymous phone call that alerted them to the fire and allowed them time to contain it before it spread to surrounding properties including a lodge for the Fultondale chapter of the Veterans of Foreign Wars.

Efforts to locate the owners of Dixie-Pro have failed.

A LOOK AT: LEVON'S HOME (LEVON CADE 8)

Chuck Dixon delivers the eighth book of the dark, action-filled series—Levon Cade.

Levon Cade is back in Alabama, home from war for good. Or so he thought…because he's called back to battle when his young cousin goes missing—a victim of a possible abduction.

Levon quickly uncovers an epidemic of young boys vanishing across the country and a conspiracy of silence to protect the man responsible.

For years he fought in all four corners of the world for his country. Now, it's time for Levon to go to combat again, closer to home—in what will be a war without mercy.

"The action is fierce an never lets up."

COMING MAY 2022

ABOUT THE AUTHOR

Born and raised in Philadelphia, Chuck Dixon worked a variety of jobs from driving an ice cream truck to working graveyard at a 7-11 before trying his hand as a writer.

In his thirty years as a writer for Marvel, DC Comics and other publishers, Chuck built a reputation as a prolific and versatile freelancer working on a wide variety titles and genres from Conan the Barbarian to SpongeBob SquarePants. His graphic novel adaptation of J.R.R. Tolkien's The Hobbit continues to be an international bestseller translated into fifty languages. He is the co-creator (with Graham Nolan) of the Batman villain Bane, the first enduring member added to the Dark Knight's rogue's gallery in forty years. He was also one of the seminal writers responsible for the continuing popularity of Marvel Comics' The Punisher.

After making his name in comics, Chuck moved to prose in 2011 and has since written over twenty novels, mostly in the action-thriller genre with a few side-trips to horror, hardboiled noir and western.

His Levon Cade novels are currently in production as a television series from Sylvester Stallone's Balboa Productions. He currently lives in central Florida and, no, he does not miss the snow.

Printed in Great Britain
by Amazon